I0541384

"We should place *The Poor Man* among the very finest of modern novels."
The Nation

"A thing of rare beauty and insight … One of the richest books we have met for a long time."
The Observer

"Miss Stella Benson's work deserves the name of genius."
The Daily News

The Poor Man

THE POOR MAN

MAN

by

STELLA BENSON

ADELAIDE
MICHAEL WALMER
2019

The Poor Man first published 1922
This edition published 2019

by

Michael Walmer
9/2 Dahlmyra Avenue
Hamley Bridge
South Australia 5401

ISBN 978-0-6485905-6-9 paperback

Cover images: Anastasya Zaplatina / RetroClipArt, courtesy of Shutterstock

I HAVE to thank the editors of the *Nation and Athenæum*, *London Mercury*, New York *Bookman* and Chicago *Poetry* for their courtesy in permitting me to use in this book verses that have already appeared in their pages.

S. B.

THE POOR MAN

KWAN-YIN, GODDESS OF MERCY

TEMPLE OF KWAN-YIN. A wide altar occupies the whole of the back of the stage; a long fringe of strips of yellow brocade hangs from the ceiling to within three feet of the floor at either end of the altar. In the centre of the altar the seated figure of the goddess is vaguely visible in the dimness; only the face is definitely seen—a golden face; the expression is passionless and aloof. A long table about 12 inches lower than the altar stands in front of it, right across the stage. On the table, before the feet of Kwan-yin, is her carved tablet with her names in golden characters on a red lacquer ground. In front of the tablet is a large brass bowl full of joss-sticks, the smoke of which wavers in the air and occasionally obscures the face of Kwan-yin. There are several plates of waxen-looking fruit and cakes on the table and two horn lanterns; these are the only light on the scene. On either side of Kwan-yin, between the table and the altar, there is a pillar with a gilded wooden dragon twisted round it, head downward. To the left, forward, is a large barrel-shaped drum slung on a carved blackwood stand.

Four priests and two acolytes are seen like shadows before this palely lit background. One acolyte to the right of the table beats a little hoarse bell. This he does during the course of the whole scene, in the following rhythm:—7—8—20—7—8 20. He should reach the 105th beat at the end of the second hymn to Kwan-yin. The other acolyte stands by the drum and beats it softly at irregular intervals. The acolytes are little boys in long blue coats. The four priests stand at the table with their faces toward Kwan-yin; their robes are pale pink silk with a length of deeper apricot pink draped about the shoulders.

The priests kneel and kow-tow to Kwan-yin.
The acolytes sing:

> The voice of pain is weak and thin
> And yet it never dies.
> Kwan-yin—Kwan-yin
> Has tears in her eyes.
> Be comforted . . . be comforted . . .
> Be comforted, my dear. . . .
> Never a heart too dead
> For Kwan-yin to hear.
>
> A pony with a ragged skin
> Falls beneath a load;
> Kwan-yin—Kwan-yin
> Runs down the road.
> A comforter . . . a comforter . . .
> A comforter shall come. . . .

THE POOR MAN

No pain too mean for her,
No grief too dumb.

Man's deserts and man's sin
She shall not discover.
Kwan-yin—Kwan-yin
Is the world's lover.
Ah, thief of pain . . . thou thief of pain . . .
Thou thief of pain, come in.
Never a cry in vain,
Kwan-yin—Kwan-yin. . . .

First priest, chants:

Is she then a warrior against sin?
On what field does she plant her banner?
Bears she a sword?

Second and third priests:

The world is very full of battle;
The speared and plumed forests in their ranks besiege the
mountains;
The flooded fields like scimitars lie between the breasts of
the mountains;
The mists ride on bugling winds down the mountains;
Shall not Kwan-yin bear a sword?

Fourth priest:

Kwan-yin is no warrior.
Kwan-yin bears no sword.
Even against sin
Kwan-yin has no battle.
This is her banner—a new day, a forgetting hour.
Her hands are empty of weapons and outstretched to the
world.

3

THE POOR MAN

Her feet are set on lotus flowers,
The lotus flowers are set on a pale lake,
And the lake is filled with the tears of the world.
Kwan-yin is still; she is very still; she listens always.
Kwan-yin lives remembering tears.

At this point the smoke of the joss-sticks veils the
face of Kwan-yin. A woman's voice sings:

Wherefore remember tears?
Shall tears be dried by remembrance?

This voice is apparently not heard by the priests
and acolytes.
Second and third priests:

Ah, Kwan-yin, mother of love,
Remember
Those in pain,
Those who are held fast in pain of their own or another's
    seeking;
Those for whom the world is too difficult
And too beautiful to bear,

All:

Kwan-yin, remember, remember.

Second and third priests:

Those who are blind, who shall never read the writing
    upon the fierce rivers,
Who shall never see the slow flowing of stars from moun-
    tain to mountain;
Those who are deaf, whom music and the fellowship of
    words have forsaken.

All:

Kwan-yin, remember, remember.

4

THE POOR MAN

Second and third priests:

Those whose love is buried and broken;
All those under the sun who lack the thing that they love
And under the moon cry out because of their lack.

All:

Kwan-yin, remember.

First priest:

Oh, thou taker away of pain,
Thou taker away of tears.

The smoke quivers across Kwan-yin's face again and the same woman's voice sings:

Wherefore remember pain?
Is there a road of escape out of the unending wilderness
    of pain?
Can Kwan-yin find a way where there is no way?

Still the voice is unheard by the worshippers. Fourth priest sings, and while he sings the acolyte beats the drum softly at quick irregular intervals:

Kwan-yin shall come, shall come,
Surely she shall come,
To bring content and a new day to the desolate,
To bring the touch of hands and the song of birds
To those who walk terribly alone.
To part the russet earth and the fingers of the leaves in
    the spring
That they may give up their treasure
To those who faint for lack of such treasure.
To listen to the long complaining of the old and the
    unwanted.
To bring lover to lover across the world,

5

Thrusting the stars aside and cleaving the seas and the
   mountains.
To hold up the high paths beneath the feet of travellers.
To keep the persuading roar of waters from the ears of
   the broken-hearted.
To bring a smile to the narrow lips of death,
To make beautiful the eyes of death.

The woman's voice again sings, unheeded, from behind the veil of smoke:

Wherefore plead with death?
Who shall soften the terrible heart of death?

All, in urgent but slow unison:

Kwan-yin.
Kwan-yin.
Kwan-yin.
Kwan-yin.

The golden face of Kwan-yin above the altar
changes suddenly and terribly and becomes like a
mass of fear. The lanterns flare spasmodically.
The voice can now be identified as Kwan-yin's, but
still the priests stand unhearing with their heads
bowed and still the passionless bell rings.
Kwan-yin, in a screaming voice:

Ah, be still, be still. . . .
I am Kwan-yin.
I am Mercy.
Mercy is defeated.
Mercy, who battled not, is defeated.
She is a captive bound to the chariot of pain.
Sorrow has set his foot upon her neck.

THE POOR MAN

Sin has mocked her.
Turn away thine eyes from Mercy,
From poor Mercy.
Woo her no more.
Cry upon her no more.

There is an abrupt moment of silence as the light
becomes dim again and Kwan-yin's face is frozen
into serenity. Then the fourth priest sings:

What then are Mercy's gifts? The rose-red slopes
Of hills . . . the secret twisted hands of trees?
Shall not the moon and the stars redeem lost hopes?
What fairer gifts shall Mercy bring than these?

For, in the end, when our beseeching clamor
Dies with our bells; when fear devours our words;
Lo, she shall come and hold the night with glamor,
Lo, she shall come and sow the dawn with birds.

Ah, thou irrelevant saviour, ah, thou bringer
Of treasure from the empty sky, ah, thou
Who answerest death with song, shall such a singer
Be silent now? Shalt thou be silent now?

The 105th beat of the bell is now reached and there
is a pause in the ringing.
All:

KWAN-YIN.

The bell is rung slowly three times. Then there is
absolute silence. There is now a tenseness in the

7

attitudes of all the worshippers; they lean forward and look with suspense into Kwan-yin's quite impassive golden face.

The lights go out suddenly.

CHAPTER ONE

EDWARD R. WILLIAMS was not listening. He was studying a tailor's advertisement in the *Saturday Evening Post* showing a group of high-colored, high-bosomed young men discussing a dog whose skin had obviously been bought from the same tailor as the young men's clothes. Edward Williams turned to a story which showed how a good young clerk served one millionaire by overreaching another and in the end became a millionaire himself, thus winning the affections of "the Right Girl."

Edward Williams felt intelligent and contemptuous—a rare feeling for him. "Makes one thank God one's English," he thought and then, because he was in the habit of refuting morbidly every statement he himself made, he thought of certain guides to British taste in periodical literature and his mind fell sheepishly silent. He looked out of the window.

I do not know how many hills lift up the dramatic city of San Francisco from the level of her sea and her bay. To the precipitous shoulder of one of these hills clung the house in which Edward sat. It was night-time and the great California stars hung out of a thick dark sky. Perhaps the stars gave the waters of the bay and of the Golden Gate their luminous look, as if there were light set in the floor of the world, a great light overlaid by fathoms of dark vivid water. Lights were spread like a veil over the hills on the near side of the bay and, on the far side, the mountains stood ankle deep in stars.

The music began again in the room. Music to Edward Williams had no connection with words or rules or understanding. He could not have been at all musical, for he never thought of saying: "You know Scriabine is clean, my dear, clean like a scrubbed olive," or, "It has been wittily said that Moussorgski is the spiritual son of Ouida and Charlemagne," or any of the things sounding rather like that, that we expect to hear from musical people as the Victrola falls silent. Edward Williams was a person of no facts at all; probably he was the only person in the world so afflicted, or at any rate the only man. Music to him was always anticipation even when it was over. Now, listening, he thought vaguely, "If the treble echoes the bass the way I hope it will, that will be too good to bear,—indeed it will be as good as I expected, and that, of course, is impossible. . . ." The treble did that very thing and Edward was blind with delight for several seconds; he breathed in pleasure; there was a sense of actual contraction in the roots of his hair.

The music paled like a candle and went out, and Edward said, "What was that?" for he was anxious to pursue that pursuing theme again across a world of scant opportunity. He would not have remembered the name even had he been told it, but at any rate nobody heard him. In America this often happened to Edward Williams.

A woman's sharp voice said, "Well say listen, what was that? It was a dandy piece." And Edward heard the man with a cocktail shaker between his knees reply, "That was the song of the twelve eagles after the emeralds of the South Sea lost their fragrance." Someone added, "They were crushed the day the love-tinker died on a hill of violets in Vienna." Edward Williams was pleased with this conversation, although, of course, he knew that it had not taken place. He knew well that he was more than half deaf and in many moods he welcomed the insight that his infirmity gave him into matters that did not exist. His two friends had been telling each other facts that both knew and that Edward did not wish to know. Neither would, of course, dream of mentioning emeralds or hills of violets except when it was really necessary and helpful to do so. Edward did not care. He felt that his mind's eye had acquired one picture the more without the trouble of acquiring a fact.

Some music that did not interest Edward began and Edward thought, "I wish I were really musical, but if I wear this grave half-shut expression everybody will think I am very musical indeed." Nobody looked at him, but he persisted in his selected expression.

Miss Rhoda Romero's pictures hung all round

the room. Of these Edward thought, "If I am
asked I will look at them in silence with a chin-down,
eye-up sort of look, as if the sun were in my eyes and
then say 'A-ha' once slowly. Then people will
think I know how good they are—if they are good."
But he never had had a chance to do this, because
nobody had ever formally introduced him to the
pictures. Rhoda Romero never asked people what
they thought of her pictures. She thought she knew.
They were mostly studies of assorted fruits in ma-
genta and mustard-colour running violently down
steep slopes into the sea. They were all called still
life, curiously enough. Rhoda Romero also, I need
hardly say, wrote poetry. It was, of course, un-
rhymed and so delicately scanned that often there
was not room in a line for a word unless it were
spelt in the newest American manner; the poems
were usually about dirt or disease, and were believed
in Chicago to have an international reputation.

Rhoda Romero herself was insolent, handsome,
and contented. Almost the only thing that she regretted about herself was that she had a great deal
of money. Her grandfather, a Mexican forty-niner,
had been so wise as to buy land all round one of
those cities of California whose motto—"Watch us
Grow"—had not been an idle boast. Many of these
cities have so far clamored for an audience under
false pretenses, and now try to justify themselves
by hanging signboards—"Drive Slowly, Congested
Business District"—on every gum-tree in the vicinity

of the lonely real-estate office. Rhoda Romero's city could have paved her studio with gold, and this, she felt, was a blot upon an artist's reputation. She thought that an artist ought to be "Of the People" and, though she had been to a very ladylike school in Virginia and had later graduated from a still more ladylike college in Pennsylvania, she used what she called "the speech of the people" whenever she remembered to do so. For much the same reason she shared a flat with Mr. Avery Bird, a transformed Russian Jew with high upward hair. They had once married in a moment of inconsistency but had since divorced each other in order that they might live together with a quiet conscience.

Mrs. Melsie Stone Ponting, tired of music, had suddenly started an argument about Art and Sex. You could tell it was an argument because now and then a little hole in the close-knit fabric of her voice occurred which was presumably filled up by some man's voice. In the United States you become used to hearing only women. Men speak guiltily in small suffocated voices. Yet arguments often seem just as spirited as though the opponent were audible. Before each clause of Mrs. Ponting's argument she opened her mouth for several seconds very widely, showing the whole of her tongue. Sometimes Mr. Avery Bird rudely took advantage of this necessity to give voice to an epigram of his own which nobody could follow.

The argument provided cover for Miss Romero

to say to her friend, Mr. Banner Hope, who was trying to make his empty cocktail glass look as conspicuously wistful as possible:

"Say, listen, Banner, I want to talk to you about You Know Whom. We'll mention no names. . . ."

Mr. Hope looked doubtfully at Edward Williams, who was about ten feet away.

"He's good and deaf," said Miss Romero; "he can't hear." And indeed, beyond a preliminary impression that Rhoda had begun a dramatic but elusive conversation about Steel Men in the Flames, Edward Williams did not hear. His protesting ears were filled with the voice of Mrs. Ponting.

"Well, say, listen, Banner, have you heard the latest?" continued Miss Romero.

Mr. Hope would have liked to be known as the wickedest man in San Francisco. He therefore could not possibly admit in so many words that he did not know the latest—(the latest sounds too wicked to miss)—so he moved his head ambiguously with a wise groan.

"Of course, I'd be the last to pick on anyone for being Bolshevik," said Miss Romero. "Bolshevism, as I said to the 'What is Liberty' Association only the other day, is the only encouraging sane reaction to a crazy world. But, you know, Our Friend here can't approach even Bolshevism sanely . . ."

"He drinks," said Mr. Hope thirstily.

"There was a most discouraging scene in Alcatraz Prison last visitors' day. He and I went together to try and say a few encouraging words to Bisley, the C. O. Edward wouldn't speak to Bisley when he got there—he said there were too many Christians banked up around him; and surely there was a considerable crowd of rather discouraging dames telling Bisley that Christ was coming—he's a religious objector, classed as Lunatic, so he has to suffer for his reputation. But I stayed in the group by way of comic relief, and Edward went glooming and snooping around. Next I saw of him he was sitting interlocked with Smith, the man who got twelve years for writing *If Abraham Lincoln Returned.* Poor Smith had a nerve-storm, you know, after he got beaten up in prison for the third time; he spends most of his time in solitary now— so discouraging. Anyway I looked around and saw Smith and Edward fairly clamped together. I forgot about them for a while until I heard a hell of an uproar, and I told Bisley, Fur Goodness sake— where's that darned Britisher?—my dear, it surely was a presentiment. For there was Edward crying —believe me, Banner, crying—that kid's got no more poise than a snake's got hips—all het up and trying to pull the hair off the prison officer in charge of the gate—one of the warders was holding both his arms."

"Why, why, why, what d'you know about that. He was stoo-ed, I guess," said Mr. Banner Hope, profoundly; but his heart was not in the matter. He began moving his empty glass about so as to catch

15   B

the light, hoping, with this bait, to catch in addition
his hostess's eye.

"Stoo-ed, you said it. He was crazy drunk. My
dear, believe me, it took me down thirty dollars to
get them to O.K. that lad's exit from the prison.
I told them how he was only a Britisher and had
gotten himself shellshocked in the service of the
Allies."

"Did he so?" asked Mr. Hope with a certain sympathy, for, before he had met Miss Romero, grown
a beard, and thrown in his lot with the 'advance-
guard of a freer America,' he too had risked his
life for his country in the course of a month in a
training camp in Texas. "Shellshock? What d'you
know about that?"

"Air-raids, my dear," said Miss Romero intensely. "Edward R. Williams survived three air-
raids in his home-city—London. I'll say he's no
stranger to War . . ."

Mr. Hope occasionally felt that he could make
a more genuinely wicked impression if he could
think of something to say. "What d'you know
about that?" he said, a little doubtfully.

"Well, say, listen, Banner," continued Miss
Romero, becoming now aware of the empty cocktail glass as her rival for his attention. "Although,
of course, personally I'm just crazy about Edward
Williams, what with one thing and another it looks
like it's up to me to get busy moving him some
place else. I'll say the Bay Cities'll get discouraged

16

with him soon. Avery and me are through with
him. I talked to him about him drinking so much
and it seemed he'd gotten around to thinking himself an interesting rebellious kinda guy, but I'll say
all his stunts look just maudlin to me; he most always
cries, and he always quits before he can put over
the interesting rebellious thing he wants to say.
Say listen Banner——''

Mr. Hope started to attention.

"I'm planning to send Edward Williams to
China."

"China . . . Why, why, why . . ."

"No, but listen, Banner, do you remember Mr.
Leung—Leung Tok Ngo—who was so encouraging
about the future of American art in the Orient?
He said the Chinese just didn't begin to appreciate
the occidental artistic ideals of today; the man in the
street in the Orient, he said, would gape at you if
you talked of Cezanne or Pizarro. Of course he
took back Benstead's Portrait of a Naked Broker
to his home in Shanghai; but that's only one, my
dear, to a population of four hundred million. Now
listen, Banner, I kinda think I'll make a genuine
United States drummer out of this Britisher . . . a
drummer of ideals, if you get me. Edward Williams
is so darn glum—he surely must be an idealist. No
real artist that I know has anything on Edward for
real bad manners, and bad manners always gets
the dilettante. I'm going to send Edward to China
with two or three dozen of those studies of mine

17

that didn't sell at the Rebel's Show. Leung is in Shanghai and can help him. I tell you I'm through with him. The Orient's gotter take its turn at him now. I'll give him expenses one way and commission, and then I quit. . . . Not that, as I say, I'm not just crazy about Edward Williams personally."

She was very direct. She left Banner Hope and approached Edward. He sat slackly on an armchair, arms forward, palms up, as though asking for something.

"Say, listen, Edward, what's your opinion of my pictures?"

This much too general opening left no room for the convention of appreciation that the careful Edward had prepared. After some thought he therefore answered, "I think they're very nice."

Miss Romero shrieked, "Very nice! Oh, Edward, you're so discouragingly British." She proceeded to convey to him the politer aspects of his banishment to China. The illusion of usefulness and a certain silliness about the plan attracted Edward, who would have refused an offer of solid travelling employment with a fixed salary. Even before he heard of the commission he said, "Right you are, Rhoda. There's nothing in the world to stop me going whenever you say."

Emily came in. She had made friends with Avery Bird without introduction at an Italian eating-house. Mr. Bird's lively yet—if the truth must be told— quite innocent friendships with women were part of the game he and Rhoda were playing. Rhoda offset them by discussing passion with all the men who came to the studio.

In picking up Emily Mr. Bird felt that he was unusually well justified. She was, of course, English, but, on the other hand, she was beautiful.

Emily had fierce, almost agonised, eyes under up-slanting brows. She had brushed her dark hair rather flatly to a smoothly wrought Chinese puzzle at the back of her head and, in the middle of her brow, her hair grew down to a little point which was consistent with the fact that every line in her face was rather keen and curious and very definite.

When Edward Williams saw Emily he thought at once, "What a miracle," and as his heart went to his throat the cocktail that he was drinking met it, so that he choked without reserve or dignity. When he recovered he found with delight that he could hear every word she said. But after his third cock-tail he could always hear well. He thought, "I wish I had reminded Rhoda that I wish to be called Reynald in future instead of Edward. Rhoda always forgets the things I want. That girl would surely look round at me if she heard somebody call out Reynald."

One of the guests had already asked Emily for a summary of British opinion on the subject of British atrocities in Ireland, Egypt and India. Emily said "You may well ask, you may well ask . . ." with great energy. She was only three days old in Californian ways, but the newcomer in the Western States becomes at once almost pathetically precocious. Yet nothing—not even self-restraint—can save him from reproach. Speech may be only silver in America, but silence is not in currency at all.

"Yes, indeed; yes, indeed . . ." said Emily, looking round nervously. Her audience noticed with displeasure that she had not yet said anything to suggest that she disliked being British. To be satisfied with an alien status implies—in the United States—criticism of the Constitution or George Washington or something. The word criticism is of course synonymous with insult. Aliens have to be very careful.

Everyone looked at Emily and looked forward to telling anecdotes later about the superciliousness of the British. But after all she had only just come into the room. Mr. Bird felt that his triumph was going wrong. "Emily is here as secretary to a very eminent Englishman, travelling with his wife to study conditions in the United States. You all know the French philosopher Moriband de Morthomme on the subject of totems and barbarians, and you'll agree with me that it applies here."

That may not have been quite the name he mentioned. It does not matter. Everyone in the room was accustomed to not knowing what Avery Bird was talking about.

"I am secretary to a saint," said Emily. She was rather vehement because she was afraid.

"Indeed," said Miss Romero with a characteristic swing of her hair, which was like a frilled red ballet-skirt round her head. "What an encouraging job. What kind of saint? There are saints and saints."

"Yes," said Emily. "Mine is both." She added after a pause, "I don't use the word in the ordinary sense which would just mean—a man I am in love with. I mean a real saint who works miracles."

"Why, how interesting," said Miss Romero. "Tell me, is he recognised by the Authorities?"

"I believe they have definitely made his reservation in the flaming chariot," said Emily. "And—oh, I do hope his cloak will fall on me."

"A bit chilly . . . flying . . ." Edward was suddenly understood to murmur into his cocktail glass.

"Explain yourself, Edward," said Rhoda Romero maternally.

Edward had just finished his fourth cocktail on an empty stomach. The blaze of Emily's eyes seemed like searchlights on his lips. "Ou, I dunno . . ." he said, delighted, "I often used to think . . . Elijah must have regretted dropping his coat like that . . . Probably quite inadvertent . . . Of course . . . central heating in the machine and all that. . . . Still . . ."

"Aeronauts say there's nothing so warm as leather," said Mrs. Melsie Stone Ponting. "An old beau of mine . . ."

But Emily still looked kindly at Edward. He had rarely been so fortunate. Everything in the room seemed to him to be brightly outlined and, though his hearing and his wit seemed to him happily alert, he could not remember from one moment to another the subject of the remarks he heard. Mr. Banner Hope was laughing almost continuously. His laughter was like something running helplessly down a slope, stumbling at every breath. Emily's saint was spoken of in the same breath as mushrooms. A miracle in connection with mushrooms at once seemed to Edward quite inevitable. Mushrooms were not logical; in fact they were made by fairies. Fairies were little saints.

"I mayn't be able to say much," thought Edward. "But I do have beautiful thoughts."

But it appeared that Emily was now talking about ducks. How enchantingly confusing.

"It was caught in the break of the waves," said Emily. "We saw it crash on the sand and struggle. They are, after a storm. So awful to have your own world turn against you like that. Usen't you to have nightmares that your mother had turned into a lion and bit you when you ran to her? I was far behind, finding out how much alike the edges of all seas are—if you pat the wet sand with your bare foot at Clacton-on-Sea or at Monte Carlo or at Bombay, it turns into a sort of trembling junket and here it was the same in the wake of a Pacific roller. Anyway when I caught up with Tam he was sitting by a broken duck. He had made it a little pillow of sand. He was holding its poor throbbing web in his hand. We waited till it died. You would never have thought a duck's beak could have assumed an expression of such utter peace."

"Say, listen," said Mrs. Ponting, "are all these tales true?"

"Not particularly," replied Emily. She added after a moment, "Well, to change the subject, what do you think of the Haiti question, the negro question, and the question of the Philippines?" There was no immediate answer to her question, so she went on rather hastily, "Well, well, fiction is much more fun than truth, isn't it? Atrocities are delicious to make up. And everyone with a great enthusiasm or a grievance lies. I met a negro called Erle Takka, who said that United States Marines strip the houses of Haitian widows and orphans and then, while they starve, stand around and prick them with bayonets to make them dance. Too frightful, don't you think, and too interesting, but—at least to a prosaic European ear—hardly likely. Up to now not a single deputation to Washington on the subject of Haiti has crossed my lips. Perhaps all this is rather superfluous . . ."

"It is rather," said Rhoda.

"It is very," said Mrs. Ponting. "I never heard such talk. Haiti indeed . . . Whoever heard of atrocities in Haiti?"

Emily was standing now and, with a feeling of desolation, Edward Williams watched her putting on a hat rather like Napoleon's. She was nervously arranging her clothes. She felt that she had been talking too much. She had a curious lapse into humility and talked in a little frightened undertone to herself. "I expect my hair needs tidying awfully . . . it's a tragedy that all lockets hang face downward . . . my bag . . . her name is Esther."

It had been a silly party. Everybody felt that —even Edward, though the party had left him a changed man. No room could be anything but dramatic to him after seven cocktails, but he realised now that the party had been silly, and that a pillar of thin air against a background of Rhoda's pictures was an inadequate substitute for Emily. For Emily was gone. Edward reminded himself that he could walk perfectly straight if he concentrated. He reached Rhoda successfully.

"Must home," he said first by mistake and then concentrated again. "I must be going home. By the way, I may change my mind about the Orient. Too far. Too sudden. I'll think it over." His own voice sounded to him very indefinite and he seemed to himself to have been talking for a long time without getting anything said. "I'll tell you what," he added intensely, "I'll think it over."

One of the most fascinating results of seven Gin-Old-Fashioneds is the disappearance of intervals between events. Before Edward R. Williams had time to think another thought, there he was looking down a precipice of street at a deliciously small Emily a hundred feet below. San Francisco streets often nose-dive like this. The grass grows between their cobblestones because nobody dares to use them except pulley cars and persons with very strong ankles. Emily was walking gingerly down. Beside her, plucking protectively but ineffectually at her sleeve, was Banner Hope.

Edward followed. If he should let himself run nothing could save him from falling like a stone into Chinatown and bouncing thence into the bay. He concentrated sternly on the alpine formation of the sidewalk, and when he reached Emily she was alone.

"Wez Bope gone?" asked Edward.

"His tram came first," replied Emily. "I'm waiting for a Ferry tram."

"Tram," triumphed Edward, who had been long exiled among mere street-cars. "That's the stuff to give 'em . . . Tram . . . Do 'em good by Gosh . . ."

There was no Ferry car in sight.

"Would-nibby fun," remarked Edward, "if we had supper at Jove Pinelli's. Night yet young . . ."

Emily paused a minute. "Yes, would-nib," she agreed.

Emily, though born in Kensington, had no lady-like instincts. And of course her mother had never actually warned her not to go to unrefined Italian dives late at night with young men fortified by cocktails to the seventh degree.

When Edward, carefully following Emily, reached a table in Jove Pinelli's sanded room he sat down, put his elbows on the table and buried his face in his hands.

"I'm too tired," he said, concentrating no longer. "You order supper." He was so tired that every channel in his brain felt sore. He thought, "I am going to die soon. If I were in a book and my present feelings were described, readers would say, Our Hero is going to die quite soon. . . . It would be luck to die in love." He suffocated with some regret his intense sympathy for himself. He looked slackly about the room and thought, "At least it is fun being so wicked. Our Hero drunk and in love on the Barbary Coast."

The room was meant for people who felt like this. Most of its occupants were simple excellent "steady beaux" from respectable homes showing their girls "Life." One young man, who no doubt had a good mother in Oakland and hid no thought from her, was singing to some friends a song which he and they believed to be very daring. "Picked it up in Paris," he said, and so indeed he had—from the Victrola in the Y. M. C. A. there. There were a few moody artists giving supper to ladies, who, though painted, looked disappointingly safe. The walls of the room, however, were decorated with scarlet devils and there were several screened grottos representing, apparently, private cubicles in Hell.

Presently Edward found that he had roused himself to say, "You know, Emily, I love you . . ."

"I know it," said Emily sadly. "I know it."

One of them would no doubt have said more, but at that moment a matchbox hit Emily on the back of her Napoleonic hat.

"Oh, hang it all," said Emily, putting down her fork and spoon. "Don't let's disappoint anyone. Let's save the Barbary Coast's reputation."

She picked up the matchbox. It was from a hotel and bore the legend—A Room and a Bath for a Dollar and a Half. "Did you see who threw it?" she asked.

"The little cad with horn glasses who hasn't shaved."

"Shall I show you what one does next?"

Edward grunted. Emily turned and smiled intensely at the thrower of the matchbox. Edward could not see the smile, but he noticed idly how prettily her hair gathered itself together for the knot, just above the nape of her neck. The thrower of the matchbox, who had been sitting with two women and three bottles, rose and came over to the table of Emily and Edward. He brought one of the bottles, but neither of the women. He said to Edward, "Say, mister, may I have the pleasure of speaking to your lady friend?"

Edward grunted.

"My name is Charlie," said the visitor, sitting down and hospitably filling first Emily's glass and then Edward's from his bottle. "Are you located in San Fran? My home-city's Seattle."

"Mine is London (Eng.)," replied Emily briskly.

"I'm doing a stunt. Round the World on a Motor Scooter."

"Gee . . ." exclaimed Charlie. "An auto-scooter! Mine's a bum job—selling Bindloss's Suspenders. An auto-scooter round the world . . . Holy Gee! And where does your husband climb on?"

Emily interrupted herself. She had already begun to answer the expected question—And how do you like America?

"Not my husband, my advance agent," she said. "He doesn't climb on anywhere. He runs behind."

"Gee!" exclaimed Charlie. "Well, say, listen. I belong to the Welcoming Committee of Seattle. I'll tell the world it'd be highly appreciated if you could put Seattle someway on your skedule and say a few words in the Wesleyan Hall. We don't get too many auto-scooter experts on this side; no ma-am, believe me."

"I'd be delighted," replied Emily. "I'll have to go to Seattle to get to Alaska, won't I? I did give a lecture once before by mistake. I was going round the world then on a Caterpillar Tractor—demonstrating it, you know. I had a mechanic and a friend on board. We passed sounds of shouting in a saloon in Dryville, Mo. My friend went in to enquire the reason and he came out presently with the chairman, having by some mistake led him to understand that we were each prepared to give a short address to the meeting. I gave rather a clever word picture

28

of Piccadilly (Eng.) during an air-raid. It was unfortunate that the English accent had never before been heard in Dryville, Mo., so I believe the meeting took my address for a farmyard imitation. My friend, a Philadelphian, spoke lucidly on the Mating of Canaries in Captivity. The mechanic was very shy; when he was finally pulled from behind the bar and placed on the platform he said nothing but 'My God.' Nobody thought to tell us until we were leaving that the meeting was really supposed to be about Seventeen Year Locusts."

"Is that right?" asked Charlie with a confused look on his face. "Say listen, ma'am. You're not married?"

"I know it," said Emily plaintively. "I know it . . . My mother often points that out to me. To my mother I am the prodigal daughter and the fatted calf is getting absolutely apoplectic waiting for me. But, personally, I love swine and they love me. Did you ever think of the Prodigal Son from the swine's point of view? They missing him so dreadfully and looking for him everywhere with little whining grunts . . . And him gone for ever. No, as you say, I am not married. Engaged two or three deep, if you like, but not married. Why?"

"Well, say, don't you want to dance?"

While they danced Edward sat and felt relieved. Always when he was alone he felt relieved. To have no effort to make was blessed to him. If anyone were with him he thought constantly, "I am surely doing something wrong." His trust in himself was always on the point of collapse. Now he thought, "For the moment I need do nothing. No one can blame me now for doing nothing. No one can laugh at me now."

He was smothering a suspicion that Emily talked too much. Would Jimmy have said, "Good Lord, the woman's a bore?" Edward would not listen to this thought.

Emily came back saying, "Well, so long, Charlie. See you in Seattle."

"You betcher," replied Charlie. He kissed her hand and returned to his naturally irritated ladies.

"Does that surprise you?" asked Emily.

Edward awoke from his moment of blasphemy. "You are so very beautiful. It did not surprise me that he came."

"No. But did it surprise you that he went?"

"I suppose he saw how absolutely furious I was getting."

"No. He danced with me. I dance very badly. I once broke a bone in my left foot and it doesn't steer very well. It's an unromantic disability, to dance badly . . ."

"It doesn't seem so to me."

Their supper was cold and tasteless now.

"I wish I could tell you how much I love you, Emily."

"You have, dear," said Emily kindly. Her fierce wide eyes were fixed upon him. They were deep set, and Edward looked with a feeling of terrifying intimacy at the shadows about them and at the diagonal prolonged dimple that led from the inner corner of her eye to her cheek. He felt he could see her thinking, "I have been rather brazen and silly tonight. You mustn't forgive me, you must love me all the better for it . . ."

"I haven't told you. I couldn't. To say anything that I could say would just make you think I loved you—just like that—that I was just one of a lot of lovers . . ."

"You don't know me," said Emily. "You only know what I look like. You have heard almost nothing but lies from me. I have only room for one true thing in my life."

"You must make room for me. When can I see you again?"

"We are going to Yosemite on Thursday. Isn't it fun? Two Ford-loads of us. Tam and Lucy and I and Avery and Miss Romero and Mrs. Ponting and Banner Hope. Now I have to catch the last Ferry."

Emily was always much affected by the skins and shapes of men and women. The last hour had been made almost unbearable to her by the fact that Edward had red spots all over his forehead and chin. I think Edward would have killed himself had he known this. As a rule he thought of those spots whenever he found himself being looked at. But tonight he was tremulously uplifted. He really

31   C

forgot that Emily could see him; he knew only that he could see Emily. If he were in a book, he thought, the spots would not be mentioned. If the book were well written the reader would now be saying, "Our hero is surely more in love than ever man was before."

He took her over to Berkeley on the Ferry. They stood on the deck in the brilliant moonlight as the boat ran out of her little cubicle under the bright eye of the Ferry Tower. The funnels and masts of other ships stuck out of similar cubicles all along the edge of the city. The ships looked like tall coy ladies in inadequate bathing tents. The moonlight was most fiercely bright. It seemed that the hills, disguised in sunlight all day, had at last unmasked. A long light cloud followed the summits of the hills so that the horizon looked like an enormous breaking wave. The air was full of lights and stars, but the water remained sombre except for a white strip spun across the bay by the moon. The noise of the water growling at the bows of the ferry so slightly occupied the silence that the screams of the trains on the Oakland side were clear to the ear. Clear to the sight were the trains themselves, little swift snakes of light pursuing one another about the bay's edge and out on to the distant piers.

CHAPTER TWO

I have sent my fires to cleanse
Away men's dreams, to devour men's
Poor dreams.
When I saw my fires, my proud
Fires lancing
A low gold cloud
I followed them, dancing.
For there is no threshold now.
No star-withstanding beams
Endure to force my pride to bow—
My pride to bow its head.
With a gold spear
I have pinned
My enemy stark
To the stars and the empty wind.
His light is dark.
His dreams are dead. His dear
And his dreams are dead.

EDWARD had long arranged to have a party next
evening. The preparations were very laborious
and dull, like those for almost all parties given by
shy and homeless young men in conscientious return
for accumulated hospitalities. Everybody in
Edward's circle had been invited such a long time
ago that no excuses had been possible. Had Edward
not reminded his friends constantly of the impending
event they would by now have forgotten all about it.

33

THE POOR MAN

In the morning at two o'clock Edward woke and realised with a sickening explosion of the mind that his party was certain to be an absolute and ridiculous failure. "Me, a host to twenty people? I can't even take the responsibility of being a good guest . . ." He had made a great resolve. "I will invite Emily."

He hoped that he would die before the party. As a solver of problems it is a fact that death has been over-rated. Edward miserably survived. He had spent three dollars out of his last few score on a room in a hotel in one of the eastern bay cities. He had missed the last Ferry home the night before. He took an unreasonably early Ferry back to San Francisco.

California mornings are very happy even if you are not in love. They fill you with happiness even if you have been drinking too much the night before. Tamalpais, San Francisco's mountain, bore the sun full in her face. Her shoulders were wrapped in a rising cloud, her mantle was rose-gold and green and, in the folds of her mantle, she boasted a steel embroidery of redwoods. The mists about the eastern hills were loosed and were blowing towards the sea. The climbing suburb of Berkeley stood clear, flushed with gardens. A glaze of golden poppies lay on the slopes behind Berkeley. The scrub-oaks grew, close as shadows, in the little canyons. There was the rare gold-green of willows against cloud-colored masses of eucalyptus.

THE POOR MAN

Californians have brought suburb-making almost to an art. Their cities and their country-side are equally suburban. No-one has a country house in California; no-one has a city house. It is good to see trees always from city windows, but it is not so good always to see houses from country windows. This, however, for better or worse, seems to be California's ideal, and she will not rest till she has finished the task of turning herself into one long and lovely Lower Tooting.

Edward stepped from the Ferry into the shrill bell-like clamor of newspaper boys. He was always outrun on arriving in San Francisco by the hard-shouldered and agile business men who efficiently caught trams on the instant of disembarking from the Ferry. Edward ran among the women and the aged and he thought, "Half of me is very nearly happy this morning. Whatever the party's like, Emily must be made to come to it. The half of me that thinks of seeing her is happy. The half that thinks of her seeing me is miserable. People are probably looking at me and saying, 'There goes a man in love.' "

All the women's stores on Geary Street were showing clothes that would have looked exquisite on Emily.

Edward left the tame urban street-car and mounted one of the wild open pulley-cars that soar up precipices to the crags where artists and Italian delicatessen merchants build their nests.

Miss Romero, in a kimono perhaps expressive of her soul, was preparing breakfast at an electric stove in the studio. Mr. Bird, in another kimono which showed a battle of sparrows on his spine, was washing last night's glasses at the sink. Their cat lay on its side pressing its shoulder blades against the sleeping Victrola. It was a parasite of a cat; it prided itself on being a member of an ancient civilisation. It never moved except to move away. It had never seen a mouse fired in anger.

"I want to ask you three questions, Rhoda," said Edward, who was not slow to notice that Miss Romero, after greeting him with automatic cordiality, managed to suggest irritation by the set of her shoulders as she bent over four nearly fried eggs.

"Surely, Edward," agreed Miss Romero. "I'm good and busy, but go right ahead. Put your questions snappily, though, A, B, and C."

"A," said Edward obediently, "I want to come with you to Yosemite. In fact, Rhoda, please, I must come with you to Yosemite."

"Dear Edward, why can't you go when and where you're wanted? Why do you have to do things so damned intensely and unlike other folks?"

"I'm never wanted."

"Shucks."

"The Britisher," said Mr. Bird, "always has to try and act unlike other folks—that's the only way he can remind us crude Colonials of his superiority.

THE POOR MAN

The Britisher is like a bull moose in carpet slippers sneezing at a poppy——"

"The American," said Edward, mildly aroused, "takes a good deal of trouble to be eccentric too. Look at all these Cults and what not . . . As a Britisher I should say that eccentric Britishers are fantastic; eccentric Americans are grotesque . . ."

"Well, for goodness' sake, Edward Williams," exclaimed Rhoda, "what's eating you? You didn't invent that dope. You stole it some place. Who's been injecting aphorisms into you?"

"Emily," replied Edward honestly. "She said it on the Ferry."

This suggestion of criticism by two aliens at once caught Mr. Bird's attention. "The Britisher," he said, "is the most complacent creature on God's earth——"

"Poor thing," interrupted Rhoda, who, having been born in the United States, was not obliged to be so ecstatically American as was Mr. Bird, who originally came from Odessa. "In the presence of God's own countrymen he just has to keep his end up some way. Do you like your fried eggs straight up or turned, British biped? Well, pass on to B."

"B," said Edward. "Will you let me off going to China?"

"But it's all fixed up," replied Rhoda. "And Melsie Stone Ponting wants you to take her kiddie across to his father in Shanghai. The father was awarded custody in the courts, but somehow she's

37

never gotten around to sending the boy. He's so full of pep she thinks he'll fall into the ocean or get knitted up with the engine the first day out."

"I can't go," said Edward. "I've got a job."

"You got a job between twelve and seven A. M.?" exclaimed Rhoda. "Well, say, listen, aren't you the bright lad? What captain of industry have you picked up with in the small hours?"

"He's picked up with Emily," said Mr. Bird. Whenever he made a statement you could see him trying to think of something smart and incomprehensible to add to it. But this time he was interrupted.

"Now see here, Edward Williams," said Miss Romero. "You can take it from me right now that there isn't a scrap of use in your starting to rush Emily. Look at Emily . . . Look at you . . . Aw, shucks, Edward, you surely are—discouraging."

"I notice that myself," admitted Edward, burying his face in his hands.

During the depressed silence that followed, Miss Romero swept on to a divan some bananas which had been posing as still life on the table and arranged instead a more formal group of fried eggs and hot biscuits. They were half-way through breakfast before she said, in the voice of one starting a new subject, "Well, say, listen, Edward, don't you want to come with Avery and Melsie Ponting and Banner Hope and me to Yosemite tomorrow? I'm just crazy to know what your reaction is to some of our National Parks."

"I do want to," said Edward.

"Melsie Ponting wants to have a talk with you about taking her little boy to the Orient, so that'll suit her fine."

"Emily," added Avery Bird, "is going with another party to another place."

Rhoda Romero was a merciful woman and, though Edward's face was so tragic as to be ridiculous, she said, "Emily will meet us at Yosemite."

"You haven't treated us to C yet," said Mr. Bird, going towards the door to show how entirely devoid of interest he expected C to be. Avery disliked most people, but he detested Edward. The view of Mr. Bird with which poor Edward was most familiar was that of his back as he sauntered away into another room. Whenever Edward noticed this he reminded himself morbidly of his own unpopularity, but apart from this he much preferred Mr. Bird's absence to his savage tongue.

"Come out with me, Rhoda," said Edward, "to one of those little beaches. . . . I am so excited . . . and unhappy. You are the only person in the world crazy enough to be good to me."

The little beaches line the southern shore of the Golden Gate. Great rocks—dragon's teeth—are sown in the sand there, and these, turned into warriors, fight the storms. The sea beats against them and the sound of it is sometimes like whips and

39

sometimes like guns. Now a rock stood between Edward and the sea. Each wave as it struck the rock threw up a fist of spray which opened quietly like a hand in the air.

"This party," began Edward. "Rhoda, I adore Emily. I want Emily to come to my party and see me at the top of my hour. And yet how shall I make it my hour? Rhoda, Rhoda, can't you save me? What kind of an hour can I have?"

"Why, Edward," exclaimed Rhoda. "Believe me, folks are just the simplest animals in the world. Nobody despises anyone without he despises himself, and nobody despises a host who pays for good unpretentious eats and drinks at any amusing dive. Why don't you think out some cute little notion to surprise us all. You've no idea how easy us folks are to amuse."

Edward retired into the shadows of his agonised soul. He tried to imagine himself introducing a cute little notion with a light roguish gesture. "Now, folks, guess what's going to happen next . . ." Could such words be uttered in Edward's husky and heavy voice? And then what would happen? Something would try to happen and fail. Edward turned simultaneously hot and cold as he imagined the scene. Avery would say something about British humor. Rhoda would be noisy and helpful. Melsie Ponting would pretend to faint on the nearest man's shoulder. And Emily——

"For I must invite Emily," he said aloud. "I

won't have a party without Emily. Please, Rhoda, help me in this matter of Emily. Nobody helps me. You don't know how terrible it is being me. It seems as if everyone were against me and as if I mattered to nobody. Yet I matter so dreadfully to myself. If you could——"

"Aw shucks, Edward," said Rhoda, not unkindly. "What's eating you? It seems like everything's got to be agony to you. Agony's your hobby, from the way you act; and you're welcome to it, for me. But you don't stop at that, you got to tell everybody how it is. Don't we all feel blue now and then without having to act a hundred and fifty per cent intense about it? If you get any kick out of feeling that way about Emily, go ahead, go right on feeling it. But have a heart and let up on agony for a while."

"Nobody's on my side . . . Nobody's on my side . . ." said Edward, standing up and clenching his fists in half-conscious imitation of Emily's vehement manner. "I'm not pretending, Rhoda; it is that I really do feel things a hundred and fifty per cent intense. Be gentle with me. . . ."

"Gentle is my middle name," said Rhoda, and she stood up and pressed a hand on each of his shoulders. "What do you want me to do, you pity-beggar?"

"Can't you see how it is with me?" said Edward. "I'm not stupid. I'm not even slow, though I'm deaf. If I'm alert and confident I'm not even very

41

deaf. But God is against me, and you are all against me, and nothing I do or say can ever be successful because there is nobody on my side to lead the applause. If I could even once come into a room and have people look up and say 'Hurrah, here he is at last . . .' I'd be a different man. I've never heard that. I hardly dare to be alive against so much opposition. My own voice is terrible to me because there is no-one who wants to hear it. I am living on a giddy high peak of unhappiness. Once before I have been a little bit in love. To my first love I never spoke—without being interrupted by Jimmy saying something far more interesting. Or if I did speak she never listened. For she was one of Jimmy's loves—and he had a dozen others in three years. I should think thirty women cried when he was killed . . . If things didn't matter to me so—I could have anything in the world I wanted. Rhoda, if I could be sure of myself for one minute—it would be worth while to be alive . . ."

As he said this, Edward saw the inner side of a long cylinder wave as it broke on a clear stretch of sand. It was the color of bright jade. The nearest wave was jade-green, and the wave behind it was a dull gold, and the wave behind that was a thick violet, and behind that ran waves of endless shades of blue. And behind all the waves stood the rust-red and amethyst hills.

"Worth while to be alive?" thought Edward. "What am I saying? I who can see so clearly . . .

Eyes in the world must always be happy, whatever hearts may be . . ."

His mind considered itself for a moment almost complacently. "In a way I must be rather an interesting feller. Lots of fellers get no kick at all out of impersonal things like colors and what not. I really get a certain kick out of being so unhappy. It is like being drunk, it makes one see more faerily . . ."

He looked at Rhoda again. She was smoking, leaning against a rock and drawing with a stick on the sand. Rhoda's strong short hair never blew out of order. The tip of her nose was never shiny. Nothing undignified ever dared to happen to Rhoda.

He donned again his extravagantly appealing look. "Rhoda, if you could let me have an hour of my own. I have never had an hour of my own. Think of all the hours you have possessed—and spare me one. Let me take command to-night, let everybody see me in command . . . let Emily see me . . ."

"Me—me . . ." he thought. "What kind of a Me would Emily want to see? . . . There isn't any cute little notion that would delight Emily . . . She would be terribly stabbing and cold to a cute little notion. . . ."

"Yet I will ride that hour," he told himself in the street-car. "It must be my hour . . ."

These were poor Edward's accomplishments.

43

THE POOR MAN

He could do two card tricks, but anyone smart could see through them.

He could sing in an unresonant voice a few of the old sea-chanteys with which Jimmy used to inspire delighted applause.

He could make paper crabs. That was rather a cute notion. But not cute enough to be the life and soul of a party. The crabs would do as a side-line. This thought enlivened his wits a little.

He could write poetry. It was unhappy, offended poetry, but not always very bad. He himself recited it at night to himself and thought it good, but he was sure that nobody else in the world would understand it.

Edward had no capacity for being comfortable. He lived in a small room in a cheap hotel in San Francisco, and in that room there was no trace of Edward except Edward himself. The room was allowed to remain an undisguised hotel room. A defaced card of advertisements and hotel regulations was on the door, a green pottery spittoon on the floor, a gaudy but not clean cotton padded quilt on the bed. Even the dirty jokes which some predecessor had written on the wall were left, and on the dressing-table was the Gideon Society's Bible, the flyleaf of which gave lists of texts to look up when business was bad or after making a successful deal.

In this heartless room Edward lived, with a telephone for his only companion. In this room that

day he sat on the small stiff armless rocking-chair
until he had made a resolve and then he spent thirty-
five minutes at the telephone.

Nearly everybody in San Francisco writes poetry.
Few San Franciscans would admit this, but most of
them would rather like to have their productions
accidentally discovered.

There was quite a decided rise in the stock of
Edward's party after he had telephoned his confused
instructions to his guests. Edward imagined all his
guests smiling tolerantly at their own folly and his.
They would hunt in the pigeon-holes of their bureaux
and bring out secret typescript. "Such nonsense,"
they would say to themselves, reading their work
with avidity and pleasure. Each guest would inno-
cently anticipate in his heart the awed silence that
would fall on the party as the last words of his poem
were read.

Edward thought that he would write a poem for
his party that would make everyone in the room pity
him. He would make fun of death. Everyone
would think, "Ah, poor soul, he has so much to bear,
he must have infinite courage." And they would
think, "He has death in his eyes. Perhaps we have
not been fine enough to understand him." Edward
thought that they would all feel a little inferior
because their health was so good. He would sit
beside Emily looking pale and brave. His deafness
would give him an air of mystic withdrawal, not
the usual air of stupidity. Nobody could ever think

45

him stupid again after his poem had been read. It would be the first hour of his life, the first hour of a new life.

But in the end he could think of no really poignant rhyme to valley, so he selected an old poem about death which he had written in the Tube in London.

Most of the guests arrived early with their poems crackling in their bosoms. Already when Edward reached the rather dirty little French restaurant between two vacant lots above Chinatown there were two motor-cars clinging precariously to the steep cobbled street outside.

Melsie Ponting and two friends were shooting craps in the low mustard-colored basement room. Melsie greeted Edward by throwing her arms round his instantly wooden form, pinioning him and making him look ridiculous.

"I brought two boys to your party to jazz it up," said Melsie. "Lon, Pike, Edward, meet each other."

Lon and Pike were already kindly pretending to be drunk in order to enliven the party. Rhoda Romero was in the room and waved flippantly at Edward. The person behind her was not Emily, it was only Avery Bird.

"I left a message for Emily. She wasn't in," shouted Rhoda. Then Edward knew that Emily would not come.

All round the table were little paper crabs made by Edward in perspiring haste that afternoon, inscribed on their backs with the names of the guests,

and brought down in a suitcase an hour before.
Nobody noticed them. Everyone sat down without
consulting the crabs. Edward cursed the crabs because they looked forlornly jocose and were not
noticed.

There were several kind persons in the room who
began to try and sit beside Edward when they
noticed him making his way to the isolated head of
the table. A thin yellow man with hair cut to resemble a wig began describing to Edward a new mouse-
trap now on sale in the Oakland hardware stores.
Edward leaned forward and smiled numbly and
thought that perhaps he was looking like a real
host.

Trays full of cocktails came in, borne by eager
dirty shirtsleeved waiters.

Emily came in behind the cocktails.

Edward pretended not to see her for a moment,
having a vague idea that this would make him more
valuable to Emily. Emily took off her hat with boy-
like indifference and, before hanging it on a peg,
waved it intimately at Edward.

"Great Scott, look at these too darling crabs.
Look, they're supposed to show us where to sit. Oh
dear, we've all sat down wrong. My crab says I'm
supposed to be Mr. Herbert B. Undressed. No,
as you were. It's Herbert B. Weinhard."

A guest called Bossy was explaining to Edward
across the bosoms of two intervening ladies his misgivings about the future of the canning trade.

47   D

"Never mind," continued Emily in a voice as clear as a flute. "I'm going to make my crab look as if it was called Herbert Undressed."

She was drawing faces on Edward's crabs. They were no longer Edward's crabs. His cute notion was simply being made cuter by Emily.

"Make my crab look like me, Emily."

"No, do mine first . . ."

"Make Edward's look like Edward . . ."

There was a great deal of giggling. The air round Emily was full of crumpled crabs. There was one in her hair. Everyone was talking now, but Edward was still entangled in the future of the canning trade. His only remark in the next fifteen minutes was, "Well, personally I never met a canner . . ." He realised at last that Bossy and he were haunted by the same fear—the fear of being left out. The canning trade was a bond between them. "At least we look as if we were talking," thought Edward. Bossy was a university instructor with fair childlike hair contradicting the severity of horn-rimmed spectacles and a little imperial. To share a danger with him aroused in Edward no enthusiasm.

"My Lord!" he heard Melsie Ponting say. "I'm just sick of sitting next to Lon. I'll tell the world he's no gentleman. He's just said something that I couldn't possibly repeat in mixed company. Would anybody like me to?"

Emily shouted, "All right then, General Post!"

48

Having arrived late she was sitting between two elderly women.

There was a deafening snarling and roaring of chairs pushed back. Everyone was changing seats. Edward sat still. It was a test of his hour, he thought, "If it really is to be my hour Emily will come and sit by me." The two women on his left hand fled. Rhoda Romero on his right hand smiled at him and moved away. Bossy moved up. Edward was suddenly filled with panic because no-one was coming to sit on his right. Everyone would laugh at him. No-one was on his side. Edward rapidly reminded himself of the few persons in his experience who had professed to be fond of him. Jimmy . . . the landlady's daughter in Putney . . . his mother . . . young Henderson at school—but he had a clubfoot . . . that amazing hatshop woman in Regent Street—but Jimmy had taken her over. . . . Quite a lot of people, Edward thought, trying to fight against his panic. "It doesn't much matter if nobody appreciates me here."

The room was dusty and hot and there were flies. A most exasperating fatigued fly could not muster energy to leave the neighborhood of Edward's lips. Dismissed, it let itself fall through the air for half an inch and then settled languidly again on his face.

Mrs. Melsie Ponting ran up the room so that the floor shook. She sat with a florid gesture in the chair on Edward's right. She looked at him with

49

her head on one side, her manicured fingers fussily arranging the beads on her breast.

"There there," she said to Edward. "Was it lonesome?" She puckered her strawberry-colored lips towards him. She dropped first her cigarette case and then her vanity bag. Edward felt smiling and busy sitting beside her. He was conscious of gratitude towards her . . . The whole room was splashing with a choppy flood of talk. Edward's ears hummed; he was drowning in noise.

"After all, I am host. It was because of me that they all came. It is only that I haven't pulled the reins yet."

"Did you bring a poem for us to hear?" he asked Melsie. "If so, you must hand it to me folded, so that I shall never know who it's by."

"My dear, you'll kill me laughing . . . Me, a highbrow? I'd swim across the bay sooner. But lots of the folks have brought things to read and they're all handing them in to Rhoda Romero. I guess it's that tin-trumpet voice of hers that makes them all think she's such a dandy reader."

She asked for something. All the time she was asking for something. She wanted a match. She wanted another plateful of the salad which had just been taken out of the room. She wanted a big coffee now instead of a little coffee later. She wanted champagne. She wanted advice about putting electric light in her garage, about whether she ought to let her little boy smoke cigars, about whether to send him to his father who had recently divorced her.

Edward rarely found himself in the gratifying position of adviser. His pleasure in the novelty, however, was partly the pleasure of revenge. "When Emily looks up this way she will see me being monopolised by another woman. Serve her right." But Emily was perversely absorbed in Mr. Banner Hope, who was singing in a half-whisper a song which he hoped was coarse enough to bring him the reputation he desired. The uncertain way in which he sang it, however, robbed the song of whatever sting it may originally have possessed. Mr. Hope must often have wished that notoriety did not need such artificial buttresses. If only some woman would commit suicide for his sake he would be a made man, but you never can count on women.

"Nobody asked Hope to sing," grumbled Edward.

"They're all treating you real mean, honey," said Mrs. Ponting. "Anybody would think it was that Emily's party."

"You're not treating me mean," said Edward gratefully. "Yet I don't know . . . Why were you so keen to sit by me?"

"Because I wanted to ask you something," whispered Mrs. Ponting. "Edward, dear, I'm just crazy to find someone plumb reliable like you going out to China who'd take my kiddie out to his dad in the Orient. For I guess I've gotter let him go. Edward, you'd never guess what a big mother-heart

I've got back of all my nonsense. My kiddie's just home to me—all the home I've got, Edward. You've never seen him but I'd just love you and him to get together—he's just a sunny-haired, blue-eyed, little honest-to-God American, tall for thirteen years —just as high as my heart, I often tell him . . ."

It was impossible for Edward not to be moved by sentiment. He was entirely uncynical. He was touched by vague reminders of motherhood and home and chubby baby-fingers and other movie properties. Yet all the time he knew that the thirteen-year-old sunbeam in question lived at a school near Sacramento which "made arrangements for board during vacations," and that he had hardly ever since he was born had an opportunity to measure himself against his mother's heart.

"I know you must be damn fond of him and all that," mumbled Edward. "It must be beastly parting with him. But you can easily get Thomas Cook or the captain of the ship to take charge of him. He'd be as safe as houses."

"Cook me no Cooks," said Melsie Ponting archly. "There's nobody to equal our Edward, don't tell me. And Rhoda says you're going to China anyway."

"I'm not going to China."

This announcement seemed to him to be fateful.

"Rhoda!" shouted Melsie in a quarrelsome voice. "You told me Edward was going to China."

"So he is," replied Rhoda with cold determination. She was very tired of Edward. He was a heavy friend, poor man.

"He says he's not going now."

"Aw, shucks."

' "Rhoda, read the poetry now," called Emily. "I'm longing to hear everybody admire mine."

> "In the darkness of my room
> I sit alone.
> I am hungry;
> I am thirsty;
> I have no fire to warm me.
> Let the stars be my meat;
> Let the moon be my goblet of wine;
> Let the burning dark sky be my fire."

Rhoda read it as though it were a good poem. She had a golden, careful voice. When she had finished she said, "I seem to have heard that some place before."

Emily added, "I think a person called Smith must have written it."

Most people were afraid that their immediate neighbors might have written it. So only one other guest risked a comment, a man with a white excited face who said, "It has no sense and nothing whatever to commend it. Speed up." His face was burning white with impatience; he was a fanatic of speed. Edward, looking at him, pitied himself because friends were so hard.

But really Edward was fortunate. About the table there were those whose presence in the position of friends Edward had not deserved or earned.

THE POOR MAN

No-one could think of San Francisco as it was in Edward's time without remembering certain faces . . . Those faces were part of the essential blessing of San Francisco.

The face of an old man in a radiance of long white hair and long white beard, the face of a connoisseur of gentleness, a face that never smiled without good cause, but in which no cause was good enough to kindle irritation.

The square keen face of the only woman in the world who can be witty even when she cries.

The face of a tyrant of benevolence; the only one of his many gifts that you must always acknowledge is his mood—if you fail to catch his mood, you offend—and perish in an avalanche of coals of fire.

Another face, sharp and changing, with the complexion of a child under careless grey hair. The face of an eager pessimist whose imagination peopled the worst of worlds with the best of men. He distrusted no man, only all mankind.

Faces of friends from whom poor Edward was too poor to claim friendship.

Rhoda read in a changed voice, with obvious serene enjoyment:

"Curse the rain.
Oh hell.
Oh hell.
The rain is zippety-zipping against the window.
Blurch—Blurch—the big drops.
Ikkle-ikkle-ikkle the little drops.
Ashes blown out of a hell of water.

THE POOR MAN

Like weasels the lightnings
Wriggle down a flat sky
After the squealing hunted wind
And the snarling thunder.
Blurch zippety ikkle ikkle ikkle.
The rain against the window
Oh hell.
I would rather wear a crown of golden thorns and find a
    pearl in every oyster on a golden
Dish
Than
Be a wet rag in a hell of water."

"That," said Avery Bird quickly, anxious to make his voice heard in the first silence, "is as full of meat as a unicorn's belly in springtime. That's real stuff."

Other people murmured, "Too wet." "Not sanitary."

The white-faced apostle shouted, "Oh, get on, get on. The next one can't be worse."

"I can't seem to get a hold on the rhythm," said an innocent Canadian broker. Edward and he had made friends because both were familiar with the same supper places in the vicinity of Leicester Square. The broker had brought his wife, a rough-hewn looking lady, whose very hat seemed to be chipped out of marble and ornamented with a wooden feather.

"It is swollen with rhythm," shouted Avery Bird. "It isn't blatant enough, of course, to allow you to hear it. It is all that rhythm can be without being metronomic."

55

Mr. Bird seemed so certain that nobody liked to contradict him. He leaned forward tapping the table angrily and glaring first at one fellow-guest and then at another.

"Speed up. Speed up."

Rhoda read again:

> "In a panic forlorn
> I am haunting your corners.
> I am dead without mourners,
> I am dead yet unborn.
> You will come to me later,
> You will come very late.
> Ah—must I wait,
>   Must I wait,
>   You unhurrying satyr?
>
> My sisters shall make
> Of their exquisite acres
> Carved aisles for the breakers
> Of sleep when they wake.
> They are strung to an answer,
> They are strung to a trance.
> Ah, must they dance,
>   Must they dance,
>   You importunate dancer?"

"Negligible," said Mr. Bird who had not yet recovered his temper.

Mr. Banner Hope added, "Woman's stuff," to show that he was a man.

Emily looked much disconcerted but she said, "I suppose it is a bit trivial."

"And foggy, too," added an alarming University student. "It has no message at all."

THE POOR MAN

"It is not worth writing or reading," said the white critic in a final voice.

"It's a song," objected Emily. "And songs needn't be messengers surely. Songs are for fancy to hear, not for brains to digest. Perhaps songs shouldn't try to have any meaning at all. They shouldn't try really to have even words. Or perhaps just beautiful words without sequence . . . silver and asphodel and Merrimac and darling and mariposa and meagre and rusty . . ."

"Well, this song tries to have a meaning and fails," said the student. He was a dark, thick young man, and his complacency, very logically, was not impaired at all by the poorness of his clothes or complexion. The fact that his collar was very high and not at all clean seemed typical of him.

Edward's heart turned cold when he thought of his poem at the mercy of that young man. He said, "At least that last poem makes a picture behind my eyes."

"It doesn't penetrate behind mine, I'm glad to say," said Melsie Ponting tartly, and many people laughed, supposing that she had said something witty. A smart voice is a great asset.

Rhoda began reading again with an abruptness which left many dazed for a few seconds.

"Damn it Jarge
 You surely do get my billy
 I asked for three silk ones

57

THE POOR MAN

And all I can find in the package is some flannel pajamas
    and one of your loveletters
By the way Harass
Has only one R.
Well the Lord goes on loving Barkeley
At least we suppose he does
We have no evidence to the contrary.
I have——"

Edward saw a young woman undergraduate's pink
face shining towards him like a sun. Her eyes
looked as though they were going to fall out. She
was waving to Edward. Edward reflected that
there were many things in the world that he did
not understand. Why should a female undergraduate with whom he was only very slightly acquainted
wave and wink so earnestly at him across a room?
Was she feeling ill? Edward blamed himself for
not understanding. "Our hero lives as if in a
dream," he thought. "Probably other men are
quite used to this sort of thing. Perhaps she is
making advances to me in a way entirely recognized
in certain circles." With his brooding eyes fixed
upon the young woman, who was now pencilling a
note, Edward listened to the poem.

> "I have had five proposals this semester
> One from an assistant instructor.
> Have you read Millie's scream
> In the Liberator for March?
> Yours body and soul
> You'd prefer body to soul I guess
> Janks."

THE POOR MAN

The young woman, Edward noticed, was, by means of signs, causing her note to be passed to Rhoda. "Notes for Rhoda but winks for me," thought Edward, wrestling mildly with the problem.

"That poet has courage," said the high-collared student. "To dispense wholly with form . . ."

"Yes, it needs courage to write that," said Avery Bird, who was narrowing his eyes and nodding his head slowly. "It is of course callow, but then so are the chickens of ostriches. Query, does it dispense with form? There is a sort of antiphony—pajamas and the Lord—the lovesick instructor and the scream—like the leeward and windward sides of a wall . . ."

Rhoda announced, "Some nameless person has just passed me a note apologising for the last poem. It was a letter really, which he or she passed me by mistake in place of a poem."

Rhoda's voice brushed the incident aside and everyone tried to look as wise as though nothing had happened. Mr. Bird, only slightly disconcerted, began to point out to his neighbor how bright was the promise of poetry in a land where even common correspondence had a rhythm of its own.

Rhoda read,

> Answer to a Friend's Letter
> "For me is such a table set?
> Shall such a gate receive me?
> For I am scarred and shamed, and yet
> Nor scars nor shame can grieve me.
> I come from a dear and desert shore

THE POOR MAN

With dancing stars my feet before;
Shall these my friends forget me, or
Shall yours—believe me?

Yet I confess that, at your door,
My stars—did leave me.

Your gates are stark and beautiful
As are the brows of Mary.
Your golden bolt is light to pull
And yet my feet are wary.
Between a sword and another sword
I see the garden of the Lord
And young saints treading in accord
A path that may not vary.

A million saints in a marching horde
But never—a fairy.

There stand the trees defensive. There
Your cautious God encloses
In a siege of lancéd lavender
Dark fortresses of roses.
Your cautious God has paved his gate
With half a score of very strait
Expensive tablets, hewn in hate
And righteousness by Moses.

How decorus, how desolate,
The art—of Moses."

As Rhoda drew breath for another verse, Edward
noticed that his poem was the next in her sheaf.

And in that second or two of silence there was
heard a curious growing clamor outside. It was
like an impossibly metallic contact of wind against

the window. For a minute everyone in the listening room had the insane feeling of experiencing something inexplicable. Then the leaping bestial yell of a fire engine approaching explained everything.

Mrs. Melsie Ponting was a smart woman. She was at the door first and, like drops from a rising mermaid, a trickle of small possessions was shaken from her as she ran; cigarettes, a lipstick, a matchbox, money, and the beads from a broken string.

"No hurry, no hurry . . ." shouted several men in laboriously indifferent voices, as the scraping chairs with one impulse shot, like splashing water, back from the central table. One man comforted many hearers by shouting jocosely, "Aw Gee, have a heart, you're on my best corn . . ."

Edward thought he would save Emily. "Our hero's first thought in danger was for his beloved . . ."

Emily was dancing about. "Oo, Edward, what a party!" She was sparkling with the pride which one feels on finding oneself present at an event. She was determined to save her hat and threw away blithely several hats which had alighted upon it.

They all arrived on the street, ashamed to have been so tense in their efforts to reach it.

The fire was in a house behind the restaurant. The fire engines were on another street, but a few firemen were keeping a space clear of onlookers on the vacant lots close by. The burning house had its back to them; it was looking away from them

61

towards the bay like one in agony turning away to bite his lips. Like a tongue the smoke hung out of one window and sparks streamed down the smoke. There was a shaking glow on the other side of the house which lighted up the low bending sky. An inverted cone of smoke spun on the roof like a top. Edward felt somehow that the whole scene was upside down, that the sky was his vantage point, and the blowing fire like a flower of the sky. The cold and usual lights of fireless virgin cities round the bay looked incredibly stupid.

He could feel the cold and usual Edward inside him saying, "My party is spoilt by this damned piece of sensationalism. My luck all over." But, "Oo, what a party," was still in his ears, and his delighted eyes were full of the fire. He was indifferent to the poems or the twenty-five dollars owing for the futile supper.

The firemen had fat jaws and looked smugly efficient, but if one half closed one's eyes and looked at them one could imagine they looked like heroes. Pursued by the dull, reluctant snakes of hose they entered the restaurant in order to turn a fusillade of water upon the enemy from an unexpected direction. Looking in through the steamy window of the basement, the delighted guests could see the bright helmets of the heroes going round the table about which so lately plates of commonplace pork and beans had circulated.

"My poem will never be read now," thought

Edward. Heroes had devoured the air in which his poem might have been read.

It was a very vulgar little fire after all. It would only have a line or two in tomorrow's *Examiner*. Quite soon it admitted itself beaten, and the perforated house sat blanketed in smoke, looking very sheepish.

"Why, what d'you know about that," said Mr. Hope, as the first fire-engine negligently moved away with a mild howl.

"Well, Edward, it's your party," said Rhoda. "What shall we do about it. I'll say it's late and not worth while to settle down again."

"Don't let's read any more poems anyway," said Edward.

Everyone began to say Good-bye in the street. All the automobiles of the guests opened their bright eyes like sleepy servants pretending they had never been asleep. To the loud snores of awaking engines Emily said to Edward, "I wish the law didn't hate fire so. It would be fun to have a garden of fire and plant little seedling fires in the moonlight . . ."

"I don't like fire. It makes a fool of one."

Edward went into the restaurant to pay for the supper. The long hot room looked tired and almost indecent. The poems were scattered about the disordered table. A fallen bottle of wine had given up the ghost pillowed on a sheaf of poems and paper crabs. Edward found his own poem—which had

63   E

been the leader of the sheaf—disgraced and brought
very low. It was on the floor, and stamped upon it
was the wet imprint of a rubber heel. As he picked
it up he saw that Emily was waiting for him in
the doorway. She came along the room towards
him.

"Edward . . ." she said in an impatient voice,
and took his arm and shook it. He could hardly
hear what she said. She looked flushed and excited.
Did she say, "It makes my life so lovely—to be
loved? . . ."   Did she say that?

Edward's thoughts were in ashes. She was watching him so insolently. He crumpled the muddy copy
of the poem and put it into her hand. He felt
nothing but an angry anxiety that she should love
his poem and that she should see how it had been
insulted.

They heard Rhoda's voice outside, "Emily . . .
Emily . . ."

CHAPTER THREE

If you were careless ever; if ever a thing you missed
In the forest—a serpent twist
Of shadow, ensnaring the starlit way of a tree;
If, at your wrist,
The pulse rang never, never, to the slow bells of the sea;
If a star, quick-carven in frost and in amethyst
Shone on the thin, thin finger of dawn, your turning away
    your face. . . .

You shall be sorry, sorry,
Sorry, for when you die
They shall follow and follow and find you
As you go through the difficult place.
The strong snake shadows shall bind you,
The swords of the stars shall blind you,
And the terrible, terrible bells of the sea shall crash and cry,
The bells of the sea shall ring you out from under the sky
In a lost grave to lie
Under the ashes of space.

MR. BANNER HOPE, although he wanted to be a
Blonde Beast, was of the type that is inevitably made
use of. He knew how to drive a Ford car. He
was known to know how. He therefore found it
impossible to demur when Avery Bird asked him
kindly next day if he didn't want to drive. It is,
as everyone knows, impossible to look personally

dangerous and daring when driving a Ford. You have to sit up straight and there is no spare room for your knees. These things give you a mincing, bourgeois look. The lady seated beside the driver of a Ford, whoever she may be, cannot help looking like the driver's lawful wife, or at worst, his lawful sister. Conversely, in a racing car with a steering wheel that bends paternally over the indolently prostrate driver, even an aunt looks painted.

Avery Bird had first asked Edward Williams if he could drive a Ford. Edward could not even have driven a donkey. He hoped that his inefficiency was a mark of temperament.

Rhoda Romero sat next to Mr. Hope, telling him of her first love adventure and criticising his driving in alternate breaths. Mrs. Melsie Stone Ponting only travelled in automobiles in order to be kissed. As soon as she was settled in the car between Avery and Edward she began obviously discussing with herself which man's arm to wear round her waist. Edward hardly counted with her as a man, still, he was unattached. She looked from side to side but there seemed to her to be no answer in Edward's eyes. So she leaned against Mr. Bird and said, "Now let's enjoy ourselves," as they started.

The Ford seemed to Edward to be a sun round which the golden planets of the hills revolved. Except for a lapse into greenness after the rains, California hills are always golden; sometimes rose-gold, sometimes lemon-gold. Now the rains were

66

almost forgotten as the travellers drove inland, but there was a faint dream of green on some of the slopes, a glaze or transparency of green laid lightly on the glowing golden hills. And, besides this dream of color, always there is a sort of dream of air between you and the hills of California, a veil of unreality in the intervening air. It gives the hills the bloom that peaches have, or grapes in the dew.

There was no need for Edward to talk or even to don the rigid semi-smile which he was in the habit of assuming, with some difficulty, when he realised that he was watched. He could not hear anything except an occasional scream from Melsie Ponting.

At four, six, half-past six and seven they stopped at saloons. The suggestion to stop always came from Banner Hope, but it did not benefit him very much, for Rhoda strictly censored anything that passed his lips. "It would be so discouraging," she said, "if our driver fell down on us."

At about a quarter to seven Mrs. Ponting began to notice Edward. She looked round from the shelter of Avery's shoulder as one looks out of a safe window at a poor man in the cold.

"Edward's shocked," she said; and then with a little shriek, "Oh boy, I'll trouble you to look at Edward's face."

"*Sir* Walter Raleigh discovering the barbarians of the Noo World," said Mr. Bird, pronouncing the

67

'Sir' with the attentive emphasis democratic America always gives to a title.

Edward had already dissolved the rigid coating of depression from his soul by means of several gin-and-vermouths. He was therefore lost in the thought of Emily and of the happier passages of his life—that dinner at Romano's when he had made fourth to oblige Jimmy with the Silly Billy Sisters . . . the afternoon on the river at Marlow when they first left school . . . Edward's happier passages were very rare and easy to remember. It was only when Melsie's attack was repeated on a higher key—("Now folks, go easy, we have a poyfect gentleman in our midst")—that he was aware of her intention.

"People don't like me," thought Edward. "They think I feel superior, but I am not brave enough to feel that. They don't know how harmless and afraid I am."

"They wouldn't countenance such things in Britain, would they, Edward?" said Mrs. Pointing. "The Britisher never hugs anyone except himself."

She shrieked with amusement and shouted against the wind to Rhoda, "Say, listen, Rhoda, we're getting good and funny at the back here—barring Edward, and he's shocked."

Rhoda looked round kindly at Edward. "Poor Edward," she said. "Say, folks, at the next saloon there's a dancing floor and an automatic piano."

In reply to this Banner Hope of course said that

his aunt in Fresno had an automatic piano too. But Edward fortunately thought otherwise. Edward's ears thought that Banner Hope said, "He could take her in two moves."

The saloon in the next town they reached had been optimistically built in the belief that the town was destined to be a Center. Perhaps the town had justified this optimism once. It was one of those towns that homesick New Englanders built in a far fantastic land of opportunity and broken hearts. Its houses, separated from prim sidewalks by hedges that were once prim, were built out of dreams of homes left behind and of domestic ideals relinquished. For one moment one thought oneself in Massachusetts, but in the next moment realised that the West had devoured all but a dream of the dream. The shell of the town was empty, cracked and even ruined. The fierce extravagance of California roses covered the damage. Scrub oak, sage brush, chaparral and prickly pear invaded the gardens of sentimental dead miners. A wild scarlet sunset crushed down all gentle thoughts of Salem.

There had been flourishing vineyards on the slopes of the low brown hills, but these were haunted now by the shadow of a date in the coming summer—the date of Prohibition. Cows were tearing the vines to pieces. Californians had given up commenting on this common and horrible sight. There were no new jokes to hide the despair.

In a row on the covered sidewalk of the town

were six saloons. The sidewalks were raised from the street level and roofed against the sun, the roofs being held up by once white hitching posts. One of the saloons was open, the others were moribund.

While Banner Hope sought a nickel with which to feed the automatic piano, the others drank a cocktail each, but Edward drank two. He did not dance. He was too self-conscious and too torpid to dance.

While the other four danced he sat at a little lame table and felt warmth and color coming into his mind. The sound of "He could take her in two moves . . ." was still in his ears. His eyes were constructing a wide red sandstone chessboard. He remembered it. Near it he was born and near it he had lived during one-third of his life. "They kept me too long in India," he thought, interpolating self-pity even with his rapture of imagination. "It accounts for me." The great chessboard was on a low hill, the only hill in a yellow seamed plain that had no limit. About the hill there was a high red wall; the indentations of the battlements were Gothic in shape. The buildings about the chessboard were like dark flowers. He could see confused flat yellow villages outside the wall from where he stood—a pawn on the great chessboard. Near him jewels caught the sunlight, and orange and blue arrows of light from the jewels pierced his sight. The knights on the chessboard wore full skirts like dancers; they looked away from their objective; when they leaped upon their crooked course their skirts swung

outward and so did their long hair. The bishops
had very thin, twisted faces and a swift, vindictive
tread. The rooks clanked as they trod, and their stiff
brocade coats were quilted. The queen's dress was
generously made and starry, and her head was outlined against the sunset. She ran like a boy from
end to end of the board; she skipped and jumped as
she drove the men she vanquished from their
squares; her laughter was as gay as frost. The
men whom she dismissed knelt and kissed the jewels
on her foot before they went. The upper sky was
the color of grapes and near the earth it was the
color of wine. Against that sky the pawn that
was Edward was content only to see the delicate
insolent outline of the queen's form. He could take
her in two moves. . . .

"The superior gentleman," said Mrs. Melsie
Ponting, sitting on his knee so violently that not
only Edward but the whole floor shuddered. She
was becoming every moment more anxious to appear
naughty and this was delighting Banner Hope, who
could now feel that he was living a deliciously wild
life without effort. It was no effort to sweep Melsie
from Edward's knee on to his own. The impulse
for this manœuvre was hers.

Rhoda Romero, though averse to the knees of
strangers and suffering from the drawback of an
innate dignity, was anxious not to seem behindhand.
She demanded a challenge to "get together" with a
couple of cowboys who had just entered and were

71

shooting craps at the bar. They wore flaring leather chaps with leather buckles, leather waistcoats over red shirts, high boots stitched in a floral design and hats of dark beaver, very broad, very high and pointed. Rhoda approached them with a rather charming suggestion of swagger and asked them where they got their hats. One cowboy answered in a low self-conscious voice, and Rhoda returned to her table with disappointment in her face.

"From a movie company," she said a little sheepishly.

Mrs. Melsie Ponting shrieked, not with laughter, but with excitement. She hoped that the cowboys would look at her but they did not. "Such is life . . . such is life . . ." bellowed Banner Hope. Avery Bird said, "Let's go," but Edward, as a defensive movement against Melsie, ordered one more gin-old-fashioned each, including a couple for the cowboys.

"Mr. Williams is wegging ub," said Melsie Ponting more kindly. It seemed to them all extraordinary that so bare a room should be so delightfully full of confusion. Everything seemed hot, and especially hot was the finger of one of the cowboys tapping Edward's knee.

"And it's not the first time either," the cowboy was saying. "I surely did draw a bum card when I got my old girl . . ."

"What got her goat this time?" asked Rhoda.

An anecdote seemed to tangle itself about Edward's exhausted understanding: ". . . a peach of a dame . . . foreigner I guess . . . gave my mare the once over . . . 'Sure, sister,' I said . . . there she was careening down the grade on my mare. . . ."

"Gadarening would be a good word for that," thought Edward.

"My God, I said, if the mare isn't acting like she was going to take the girl home to my old girl . . . and sure 'nuff. . . . This foreign dame I'm telling you of rides back . . . kinda queer her way of talking was. . . . 'Your wife's after me and you,' she says . . . and back of her, sure 'nuff, come the old girl. . . . She was bluc's a lemon when she got here. . . ." He broke off. "Well, presence of ladies . . ." he added, smiling fatuously. "Her language . . . sour as a lemon she was, yapped like a coyote. . . . And the foreign dame laughed . . . put her head down and kinda sobbed for laughing . . . *she* should worry . . ."

"I believe it was Emily," said Avery Bird suddenly.

"You betcher it was Emily," agreed the cowboy, realising that his story was improved by this fact. "It would be. Emily for mine every day of the week not forgetting Sundays. . . ."

Edward and the cowboy inadvertently walked out hand in hand. The cowboy retained Edward's hand even while he affectionately shook the hand of every other member of the party. The trees and the houses and the cowboy suddenly slid away to the

73

re-awakened tune of the Ford's engine. Only the stars and the moon accompanied the party.

They drove the car at last through a gate into a broad moonlit hayfield. It was like a stage set and lighted for a great ballet. There were no dancers but the moon and the haycocks. All the haycocks bowed before the moon.

Rhoda and Melsie chose a haycock against which to spread their blankets. Avery Bird and Banner Hope burrowed into another haycock. Edward, by himself, chose yet another. He arranged his blankets and then stepped back with his head on one side like an artist. There never was seen such an exquisite place to sleep in. In different parts of the field the others were singing, catching an infection of song one from another.

"Oh dig my grave both wide and deep . . ." sang Edward hoarsely.

When he lay down the upright blades of hay moved in the breeze against the sky. There was one that was like a pen writing upon the sky.

"In an hour and a half I can say, 'Today I shall see Emily,' " he said. But in an hour and a half he said nothing. He could hear an owl through his sleep, but he said nothing.

The line of sunlight, as Edward woke, was climbing down the opposite hillside as the sun fought its daily preliminary battle with the eastern mountains. On the near hillside, pine tree after pine tree flamed in the descending green light. When the woods that bordered the fields achieved their morning, shafts of gold dust slanted between the trees. There was a dark brilliant red in the shadows of the woods.

Cinders in hot cakes taste glorious under an early sun. Mrs. Ponting was sleepy and a little more kind than usual. She sat plaiting her hair and giving directions to the men while Rhoda efficiently cooked hot cakes. Edward, who had walked a very long way into the forest in search of wood, returned with half a dozen twigs and with news of a bear's track which he had discovered in a patch of wet sand by a stream—the great print of the palm and three precise dents for the claws. The fire was so fierce under the frying pan that his characteristically poor contribution was devoured in it like a War-savings Stamp in the cost of the Great War. But he thought; "I can tell Emily I heard the bear crackling in the undergrowth. I might say I couldn't swear to it and then it wouldn't be a lie. Anyway she is a liar herself. But liars don't necessarily approve of liars."

They all sang during half the day. Along the road which followed the pale green foothills they sang; the squirrels, escaping to the embrace of mean and ragged foothill pines, clasped their hands upon their breasts in pious surprise as the loud song passed by to the kettledrum accompaniment of the Ford. The heads of gophers shot out of their holes and in again, till the slope bubbled with half-seen creatures in the sun, like boiling water. A snake oozed like quicksilver across the road.

Higher and higher. The steep slopes were heaped with dogwood and buck-eye and awakening azaleas. Mariposa lilies stood in the cool shadow. A couple of deer waded in the lilies. Sometimes a web of cloud-blue lilac was spun from tree to tree. The dark wine-colored Judas tree was nearly over.

The forest presently closed about the travellers. They were prisoners. The very passing miles held them closely prisoners. The trees were wrought steel bars between them and their sunlit and delirious cities. The noise of the car was beneath the notice of the silence. The silence of the forest was much louder than their voices or than the stuttering of hearts and engines.

Their eyes leapt absurdly and inevitably up the shafts of the trees. When the striped earth sloped the trees sprang at one angle from the slope like javelins thrown against one enemy, the sun. The sky seemed stabbed by the javelin trees. The high down-pointing cones were barbs, closely embedded in sky.

The sunlight stood in fluted slanting columns hardly more ephemeral than the trees. There was an obsession of trees in Edward's mind. Out of the corners of his eyes he could see an unceasing bustle of birds and squirrels and insects among the trees, like a hinted joke on lips that were sealed when he looked directly at them. Everything was secret.

THE POOR MAN

A few acres of the forest were secretly and quietly on fire. It was the spirit of fire with its eyes shut, intensely malevolent. There was but little flame; a little dagger of flame or two, as though the keeper of the savage secret could barely refrain from committing himself. Blue smoke curled from the roots in the ground; thin snakes of smoke writhed about the innocent strong trunks of the trees. The air was hot and the hanging pale scarves of lichen waved in the heat. It was an intense relief to leave the smoke behind and pass through the living, unthreatened spaces of cool forest again.

There was a pause in the day at the foot of a monstrous horned tree. An experiment on the part of the Creator but not, Edward thought, a very successful one. Trees should be young and shining or they should be immortal and carry their age like a gentle green dream. The greatest sequoia of all is a horned devil with a senile brow. The weight of his thousands of years is like a torpid curse upon him. One thinks miserably of his contemporaries, Moses and the jewelled Pharaohs, and one is glad that the ancients died decently and thoroughly and are only very sparsely survived. Some of the trees on the slope—younger by a thousand years or so—were very much more splendid. The grain of their rough and rusty bark ran up in slow spirals—for ever, it seemed. No great branches drew the eye away from its climb upward to the tapering spear of the tree. Only, far up, near the sun, the little delicate branches and needles sprang out and shone like the drops of a fountain.

"Why, why, why . . ." said Mr. Hope, after reading the notice board at the foot of the horned tree. He gave the tree a quick congratulatory glance and said to Edward, "Say listen, you don't get trees like that where you come from."

Edward's mind ran home. "No," he agreed vaguely. "Not trees like this. No notice-boardy trees like this. Primroses, of course, and what not."

"Your notice boards in Britain," said Avery Bird, "say 'Trespassers will be shot at sight,' or something very like it. Our notice boards in California say 'See here, folks, come and look at this tree,' or some such thing."

"That's true," admitted Edward. Still, it's more fun to disobey a notice board warning you off than to obey a notice board calling you on." I am not sure that he really said this. If he did I do not think anyone heard him. After a second or two he realised at any rate that he might have said it and he thought, "Really, you know, I am quite clever. Only Emily is never there when I am clever. Nobody is on my side. There is nobody to think, 'Well, by Jove, our hero is not so very unworthy of his Emily after all. . . .'"

The grotesque dance of the Ford car between the quiet trees began again. Back and forth, back and forth, along the climbing roads it toiled. Higher and higher. There were patches of old crusted snow beside the road now. The little meadows among the trees were extravagantly green. The very shadows were green.

The earth opened before them. There was suddenly nothing at all between them and another world. The faces of the opposite mountains—El Capitan, Half Dome—were made gracious with Gothic curves. There were far mountains—red mountains, patterned with snow—to the east of the Half Dome. They were like still flames in the low red sunlight. Yosemite Valley was filling with blue shadow as the sun went down. The line of shadow climbed up the sheer cliffs like rising water and overflowed the tall shallow arches of the cliffs.

Edward thought, "I can't bear to be alone with this. One can't be anything but alone in such an indecently enormous world. There is nothing that will ever come near enough to save me . . . Unless Emily would come . . ."

Avery Bird said, "The other party ought to be quite a short ways from here. They'd planned to wait for us before going down into the valley. Let's all call Emily, let's sing Emily all through the woods."

"Emily . . . Emily . . . Emily . . ."

They moved along the shadowy road. The sunlight slipped from the brim of the lower cliffs across the valley. The brows of the mountains were still alight.

F

"Listen," said Rhoda, and Mr. Hope, listening to excess, stalled the engine by mistake.

"Hurray . . . Hurray . . ."

It was a very small distant voice. There was a very small distant Emily framed in tall trees. It seemed to Edward that all the trees they had seen had been but an avenue leading to Emily. She was waving violently at them with both arms. She ran towards them.

"A deer came and almost kissed me," she shouted urgently as she ran. "We didn't light the fire till now for fear of frightening it. The darling thing. We are going to have four fried eggs each. We bought all the eggs in the last town."

"I guess you got to admit now that London has nothing on this," said Banner Hope.

Leaning over a doubtful camp fire knelt Emily's employer and his wife. Emily danced about them without dignity. "Isn't it fine? Isn't it fine? Soon it will be all starry above and we shall be just seeing each other's nice faces and eating four fried eggs each."

"You spoil things by expecting them too much, Emily," said her employer, snatching facetiously at her dancing ankle.

Tam McTab, that eminent journalist, had a large dark complacent face. His eyes, unexpectedly, were very pale grey. They were like lapses into vagueness in a vivid face. He had straight black hair, the front lock of which seemed grown at a different angle from the rest and either fell obliquely across his forehead or was blown upward by the wind. He had rather a fat, satisfied chin. He stooped, not so much with slackness as with alertness, as though he were leaning forward to catch the sound of something passing.

His wife, Lucy, had a round, rather indeterminate face and pale drooping hair. Her clothes made her look collapsible and boneless. Even her hat was draped rather than set upon her head. Her lips looked stiff as though she were biting them constantly.

Edward knelt at her side and looked at the fire rather helplessly. He lit several matches but they went out without doing any good. Rhoda Romero took command.

It was dark at last and the stars crept in procession across the space of sky above them. The fire, a slowly spreading ring of fire rooting itself among the pine-needles, was between Edward and Emily. Lucy sat beside Edward.

"Are you fond of reading?" asked Lucy nervously of Edward. She was trying to make a little safe alcove of conversation in the great silence that stood about them. She had not intended anyone else to hear her; she was obviously not really anxious to know whether Edward was fond of reading. But she was accustomed to rooms and to a polite murmur of talk.

Emily heard her and said gushingly to Tam,

"Do you play tennis, or is blue your favorite color?
Lucy has brought the drawing-room even here.
Lucy, won't you even take off your hat? Is it because of the angels? St. Paul's angels aren't in the
forest, surely."

Edward was hardly ever scornful except of himself. He knew too well the difficulties and dangers
involved in being alive to despise those who sought
for safety in tremulous platitudes.

"I write more than I read," he admitted in so
low a voice that even the mocking Emily could not
catch it. "I don't write well, but I love writing."

"Oh, how clever of you," said Lucy. "I'd have
loved to write but I never could at all, I'm sure.
It's a gift, isn't it, really? Tam writes wonderfully.
But then he does everything well. He reads a great
deal too. He often says he doesn't know where he
would be without his books. He reads wonderfully
well aloud. Even here he has brought books.
What is the name of the man who wrote that sad bit
of poetry—the 'Song of the Shirt?' George Moore.
I saw some books of his in Tam's suitcase. I always
tell him—half in fun, you know—camping isn't the
place for reading. I admire scenery awfully, don't
you? I am a very observatory person—I often
notice things that Tam missed altogether, and then
I tell him and sometimes he puts it in his books.
That is to say, he did once . . ."

Her uncertainty robbed her manner of the slight-
est trace of enthusiasm. She bit her lips and looked

at Edward to see if he was listening. She seemed
to be chronically unflattered.

Edward felt ease and complacency covering him
as she spoke, just as he felt the warmth of the fire
enveloping his happy body.

"Yes, I love looking at great things," he said in
a proud throaty voice. "I am myself no reader
anywhere, out of doors or indoors."

Emily was still rudely listening. Nobody else
seemed to be talking. Emily was laughing a little.
The low fire made a poppy-yellow light on the point
of her chin, a theatrical light. A duller light was
on the soft silk shirt that followed the gentle lines
of her breasts.

"I have got an idea again," said Emily, thumping
the pine needles excitedly with both her hands.
"Oh, now I come to think of it, I can't say it so that
it sounds a very good idea. It's about being honest.
Did I talk about it before?"

"Yes," said Tam, and Emily's body relaxed with
disappointment. Edward thought that Tam was as
hard as concrete and that certainly Emily would
never bear to be laughed at or to be beaten at games.
He was quite sure that she would behave badly at
games and contradict the umpire.

"Well then," said Emily rather lamely, "I'll talk
about it again. Don't you think it's tremendously
interesting to make people be honest against their
will? To startle people suddenly into being honest
about their standards—about why they cry and why

they laugh and when they lie and how much they pose? Posing especially. Although everybody poses, only about ten percent I should think laugh secretly at their own poses. People's poses make them slow to admit, for instance, that they laugh only when there is something a little dirty in the joke, or that they cry when their conceit is wounded, or that they powder their noses to attract men and not for the health of their complexions, or that they lie. Let's all pose as being absolutely honest. Lucy, quick—how much do you lie?"

Lucy bit her lips. She made a little tower of sticks at the edge of the fire and tried to convey a little torch of flames to the tower. "Why, Emily, don't talk like that. I try not to lie at all, of course."

"Oh, I try frightfully hard to lie," said Tam. "I am always deeply disappointed if I do not succeed in deceiving everyone I know about what I am and what I have whenever I want to." He spoke of himself with great confidence and with an obvious certainty that whatever he chose to say about himself was interesting. One felt that he would just as complacently have explained that he always used Vinolia Soap or that he preferred silk socks to woollen ones.

"Oh, you naughty, naughty man!" said Melsie Ponting. "As for me, I only lie to make a funny yarn funnier. I never mean to deceive a fly."

"I lie to save myself from myself," said Edward. He thought this sounded modest and tragic.

"I lie when I am angry or when I am frightened," said Rhoda. "If I were always calm I should never lie at all, I guess. Except that I never tell anything that happened to me exactly the way it happened."

"I have no conscience at all," Banner Hope said. "I remember when my Momma used to catch me stealing the candies . . ."

"Truth," announced Avery Bird, "is a bastard begotten by a steam-locomotive and born of the scent of jasmine— if you get me. Truth is the ghost of a decadent vice, clanking steel chains; Mary Magdalene was crucified on truth instead of a wooden cross——"

"Oh, for the land's sake, Avery," exclaimed Rhoda. "Do you have to act so damned complex? Nobody gets you, believe me. It's because he's a Jew . . ." she added apologetically to the others as she took Avery's hand.

"I think you're all posing," said Emily. Her clenched hands became slack, as though with disappointment. "If I began to say how much I lied I should pose as a miserable sinner. Yet I do lie, to save myself from the anger—which I deserve—of other people. And I lie often in order to seem uniquely honest. Oh, hang it all, there's no getting away from pose after all. We're all posing as liars now because it's more popular and funny to be liars——"

"Lucy didn't," said Tam, as though Lucy were his property.

Emily interrupted, "It was the talk of reading and writing that reminded me. While I was lying in the sun before supper I tried to read George Moore's Confessions of a Young Man. I thought Tam would presently ask me what I thought of it and I began trying and trying to think of something clever I could say—something that would sound so clever that even Tam wouldn't dare to strip the skin of cleverness from what I should say and see how light and womanly was the core of my thinking. And then I thought it would be fun to say to myself what I really did think, not trying to show off. So I read the book with one hand and wrote everything that occurred to me with the other."

"Well, I suppose we'd better hear what you wrote," said Tam, knocking out his pipe in a jovially resigned way.

"Tam, don't you really want to hear?"

"I see you are determined to let us hear."

Edward thought, "I certainly have no delusions about her. I can see that she monopolises talk too much. And she talks entirely about herself. Having no delusions about her I can see the more clearly how adorable she is."

"When I read my notebook now it is like a fog

translated into words. Yet I swear this is all I thought about George Moore, and I am not abnormally stupid."

"No indeed," said Banner Hope helpfully.

"This is what I find in my notebook:

'Why not die if you are Victorian? *Terrible is the day when each sees his own soul naked.* But his soul is all dressed up in tight trousers and what not. And side-whiskers. I wonder if my navy shirt is too tight? My mind is wandering. I must read this book acutely. *I fain would show my soul.* Mrs. Felicia Hemans toying with adultery. My first schoolroom had a green wallpaper. What's this about Scott. *Too impersonal.* Who cares for the effect of Scott now? Might as well care for the effect of Little Arthur's History. Oh, what roguey rogue he is trying to be. *Of course I liked the fashionable sunlight in the Park, and to shock my friends . . . I boasted of my dissipations.* Now he boasts of his boasting and that is just as bad. *A satyr carrying a woman.* How laboriously luscious. But why not laboriously luscious? He's got to give his Young Man something to Confess. But in these days we would laugh at his Young Man. Because he isn't young. He's only pretending to be traditionally young. *I cannot recall a case of man or woman who ever occupied any considerable part of my thoughts that did not contribute to my moral or physical welfare.* He is very proud of that.

THE POOR MAN

He thinks that using people makes him great. Men are vainer than women. Or naïver. Talking of vanity, I'd like leather buttons on my coat like a man's. They would look sort of tawny. *Beginning to regard the delineation of a nymph or youth bathing as a very narrow channel to carry off the tide of a man's thought.* How very good all this is. How honest of him to admit his impression of Impressionists. The shocker shocked. Hurray. He is not a spirit shocker but a flesh shocker. It is certainly fair of him to admit his vulgarity—if only he knew how vulgar it was. I don't know about all this. I don't know Théophile Gautier. I am a fool. I am a woman. Why do they let women be like me, skipping the strange parts of books? I think the needles on the pine trees are woven like Japanese matting against the sky. I am bored. I am bored. Now I am not bored. I am proud of being not bored; I am proud because the quotations from Gautier please me so. I am applying it all to myself. Oh, he is laughing at me. Being a woman, that's the trouble. *Pity, that most vile of vile virtues, has never been known to me.* Is it being a woman that prevents me from understanding how pity can be vile? Women are paid to pretend to understand men's epigrams. Epigrams about virtues are easy. Pity isn't really vile, only there are three sexes, men, women and people who pity. *It is said that the tiger will sometimes play with the lamb. Let us play.* He is laughing in a laboriously aesthetic way. He is pulling the nineteenth century's leg, but the twentieth century can pull his. It is all Victorian smart like a minor novelist's club. Affectations of an out-of-date "deliciously naughty fellow." Written for sheltered women. *The real genius for love lies not in getting into but getting out of love.* All right. But does the word love catch every woman's eye as it catches mine? *Pythons . . . Persian cats . . .* Are men then really so naïve? No woman would bother to retail such Garden Suburb vice. Or do I not understand the joke? Yes, I know he wrote it when he was young. But he re-published it when he was old. Has he not noticed what has happened to the world since he wrote it? It is re-published in fun . . . as a survival. If I were cleverer I would have been laughing all along. But it is proud of its Bohemianism. The game of being a Bohemian can only be played with a smiling mind. You can't have a smiling mind among Pythons and Persian cats. No— *Hypocritical reader, in telling you of my vices I am only telling you of your own, in showing you my soul I am only showing you your own.* When he talks of readers and souls and vices like that he is using a dead language. The reader he apostrophizes is dead. He has the sustained smirk of a John Leech "Toff." He is an inverted Pollyanna. Now I am in America. We don't pretend now. We don't leer. When we leer we see ourselves in the glass now.'

89

Tam McTab said, "By Jove, Emily, you ought to be shot. You are terrifying. You are too conscious, you frighten one."

"Tam, do I frighten you? Tam, say quickly, do I frighten you?"

"Not so much as you might," he said. "Because we are all somehow metallically unsimple in these days. I am too. We can't even be naked without noticing it. We can't even think without thinking about thinking. But you are too unsimple to be allowed to live, really. It is simple and human to pose a bit and not to know you are posing. When you try to know yourself so well you devastate yourself. You are conspicuously inhuman even in an inhuman age. You are too hard-hearted to have delusions and to make mistakes and love yourself peacefully as everyone else does. If you hit nails on the head you do it savagely, with a purpose, and kill something with it—as Jael did."

It was suddenly apparent that Emily was crying, but she made no sound and said no word. Her eyes looked round and strained and the firelight caught the tears on her lower lashes.

"Is that a bird calling?" asked Lucy mildly. Lucy's cindery hand was nervously poking the fire with a twig.

Information was generally left for Rhoda to give. "It is not a bird. It is a man whistling."

The firelight glared suddenly and cast all their shadows outward in a circle. Their shadows were like the petals of a dark flower with a flaming centre.

They listened to the sound of approaching steps across the soft pine needles. Edward listened but he could not hear. A panic seized him because he could not hear. "Probably the forest is full of great sound. They talk of birds and whistling. The world can't be nearly as still as my world is. My hearing reaches no further than the light of the fire. I have no impersonal hearing at all. Perhaps they can all hear that waterfall across the valley and perhaps owls and the tread of deer. I should be ashamed to tell Emily how little I can hear, although I can always hear her voice. I am defective. Our hero in a tragic mood of self-realisation. Our hero indeed! I am not even my own hero."

He drew back a little from the dancing light of the fire because he wished to have shadow on his eyes which were filling with tears of self-contempt and self-pity.

"Real men never cry," he told himself. "What is the matter with me that I have never grown up into a man? Here are two men coming out of the forest. They need a shave. They have big muscles under their skin. Even when they get drunk they probably never cry and surely they never hate themselves. I don't love Emily—as either of those two men could love her. I love her deafly and drunkenly and neurotically. Is there no happiness at all for poor things?"

The two unshaven strange men he was looking at stood in the outer radius of the firelight. It
was amazingly unlikely that they should have found
the campers, it seemed. Edward thought that he
and Emily and the others were like bees hidden in
their flower of flame and shadow. But now they
were found.

"Any of you folks got a match?" asked one of
the strangers. He added when he had lighted his
pipe, "Why, you're San Francisco folks, aren't you?
I know because I had the pleasure of listening to
you, Miss Romero, addressing a meeting of the
What is Liberty Association last week. Say, did
you know the office of the W. I. L. A. had been
raided? Sure it has. I wouldn't of known it only
that I happened to be right there on the stairs when
the police hit the place. Took my name and address
and showed me the door."

"Why, what d'you know about that?" murmured
Banner Hope. Rhoda looked rather white.

"Have a drink, strangers?" said Avery Bird.

CHAPTER FOUR

Ah, fortunate,
Ah, fortunate . . .
I can defy tomorrow's law;
Never tomorrow can say to me—
It passed you by. You did not see.
For I saw. . . .
There was a star fell out of the night,
Fell down that tall blue precipice,
And I had time to lift my sight,
To lift my fortunate sight to this
And say—I am not too late,
I am not too late.

DAYS and nights went by under the trees. The travellers went down into the Yosemite Valley itself. At one hour the subtle shape of Half Dome was suggested through a robe of morning mists, at another it was hewn starkly out of a hard sky. They confronted the incredible grained and golden face of El Capitan, that perfect half of an unknown whole, that perpendicular desert of stone which bares its naked heart to the sun and whose boundaries march with those of the clouds. There was for days a sound of falling waters always. Edward did not hear it, but he could see the thin silken bands of water binding the mountains, and he could lie at the feet of falls in an explosion of light spray and

93

watch the stars shoot out of the smooth high brim of the fall three thousand feet above him.

The red pine ground was their bed between the crimson and golden trunks of trees. There was always light on the river and often, it seemed, a light within the river, a twisting snake of light.

Yosemite was printed like a dream upon that part of the memory that registers impossible things . . . .

They were motoring westward again through the gold country—Eldorado. The two Fords were together now, Tam driving the first. Lucy was in the front seat beside Tam. Emily and Edward sat in the back.

"I have never really driven a car before this trip," said Tam as they started. "In England I am no motorist, though a friend's Rolls Royce occasionally wears Lucy and me as buttons. But I am no driver and it alarms me to have anyone but Lucy in the seat beside me."

Lucy looked at the country with a patient expression. The angle of her head followed the line of the hills. The line was like a feverish temperature chart against the sky and Lucy watched it with uncritical attention.

Emily put her hand upon Edward's thin arm. "You know, Edward," she said, "you're a masochist."

"I suppose I am," said Edward despondently. "What is it?"

94

"A person who enjoys hurting himself."

Edward considered this.

"That's what makes me want to love you without being loved," he thought. "Yes, I want that. I want to be hurt and to make myself sick with pitying myself. I want to ensure that you shouldn't love me by telling you the worst about myself."

He found it suddenly a real effort to be silent. He wanted to tell her how unhappy he was; he wanted to try and make her cry for him, or rather to satisfy himself that she would never cry for him. He wanted to tell her how often his head hurt and how poorly his ears served him and of the unbearable thundering and crashing that was always in the foreground of his hearing. He wanted to tell her how impossible he found it not to drink too much, how impossible he found it to be like other men. He wanted her to say, "Poor Edward, poor man . . . " and stroke his hand.

He said, "Emily, are you really as hardhearted as Tam says?"

They both looked suddenly at Tam. He was telling Lucy in his usual absolutely confident way of some small experience of his own—an experience that would not have been worth describing had it not been for his own intense interest in it. They heard him say, "And the silly part of it was that if I hadn't been wearing those old grey flannels the feller wouldn't have dared to speak to me like that."

He had a habit of speaking to Lucy as if she were not his wife but a friend.

Emily leaned her head suddenly on Edward's shoulder. "How can you be so brutal?" she said. "How can you ask me if I am hardhearted when I am in such pain—and all for love . . ."

She never could keep her hands still. She threw out her right hand as if in surrender and hammered the side of the car. Edward could feel that she was absolutely tense. The muscles of her neck were unyielding.

He thought, "I must be very cautious." He understood that he was not in Emily's world at all. "I must be very cautious even in thinking of her now . . ." It was like falling into very cold water and becoming at once numb. "I mustn't be feeble in this too. I must be a hero in another way. If I love her without hope, in the end I must die because the pain will grow and grow." He looked forward almost eagerly to atrocious pain forever. The forever of the morbid introspective is not a real eternity. I believe he looks forward in the very end of the end to telling God and being publicly pitied and caressed at last. "Well done, thou good and faithful servant, thou hast been alone and unfortunate in all things. Enter thou into the unending pity of thy Lord."

The wind blew back to them something that Lucy was saying. "Well, it's just as I always told you, Tam. You never know what you can do till you try." They were being briskly polite to each other. They were what is called in sprightly domestic literature, "Good Comrades."

"When you asked me if I were hardhearted, Edward," said Emily, "I suppose you were going to tell me something about yourself."

"I was," replied Edward. "But I won't now. Anything I could say to you now would seem too big to me and too little to you. My love, for instance. And the fact that I must miss everything in the world . . ."

"Your deafness . . ." said Emily. "I gathered you were a bit deaf even before Melsie Ponting told me you were as deaf as a post. Tam said— 'Yes, and as slow as a Sunday post'—but I told him to shut up. It must be beastly being deaf because I suppose you feel that you seem stupid and that people get tired of talking to you. Why don't you go to a doctor and all that? I always go to doctors the very minute I have a symptom—doctors are so awfully interested and lean forward when I talk about myself, which of course nobody else will ever do. Other people tiresomely begin talking about themselves as soon as I get going, but luckily doctors never do that. Tam is the only person I know who can talk successfully about himself, but then he is always perfectly happy about himself and talks of what happened when a vital button came off at his wedding, or how pleased somebody was to see him when he called, or why an Armenian mistook him for

a Turk. And everybody listens with a poised smile
on their lips, and when he has finished there is always
a loud noise of success. Sure and happy people
never fall flat. Edward, if you weren't so sad-
hearted, people would love you much more."

"That's what happy-hearted people always say,"
said Edward. "Happiness and sadness are not at-
tributes and not moods. They are the foundations
on which people are built. You can't change your
foundations."

"Well, if you are sad, your castle is built on
sand. It is so safe to be well and truly laid on a
happy and a rocky heart. Then even pain is nothing more than storms beating on the rock. When
the storm goes down you are wet and perhaps a
shade chipped but still safe."

"I am never safe," said Edward. "Never safe
for a second."

"Oh, I am so tired of talking about you and me,
Edward dear," said Emily sitting up.

They were silent and Edward felt as if he were
learning Emily's face by heart and as if it were a
lesson knowledge of which would be most urgently
required of him some day. Her upper lip was
thinner than the lower and, though the upper lip did
not protrude beyond the lower at all, the effect of a
little uptilted pout was produced by the line below
her mouth which receded very definitely before jut-
ting out to form a rather large round chin. Her
nose was strong and rather broad, absolutely

straight in profile and a little tilted. Tilted lines were necessary in her face to support her slanting thick black brows and the upward angle of her dark hair. She was smaller than most people and looked as if she were accustomed to putting her shoulders back and looking half defiantly up into the eyes of large, strong, delighted men.

There were no level places in the land they were passing through and no color except a hot brown. The air shook in the heat; the summits of the brown dead hills seemed to be seen through shaken water. There were scars in the hills made by old gold-seekers here and there, and surviving one-man mines stabbed the slopes. Small villages of bleak grey shacks clung to the road. The sunset turned the brown to red; the air in the shadow of the hills was russet red. It was time to find a camp site. Whenever they turned a corner and looked down, as it seemed, upon a perfect site, some little town had chosen that site too. There was no remoteness in that strange broad land.

"This damned country has broken out into a rash of towns," complained Tam.

One of the intrusive little towns seemed to attract the sunset. Its windows flamed in orange; its roofs smouldered in dull crimson.

"It's like as if it was on fire," said Lucy. "Stop, Tam, and let me look." Lucy always had to look where the others only glanced.

"Lot's wife," said Tam.

99

"One thing, by the way, that we know because the Bible tells us so," said Emily, "is that Lot didn't care a damn for his wife. If he had cared he would at least have looked round at her predicament; probably he would have tried to help her or melt her or something. We should have known if he had because he would have been preserved forever as a pillar, a monument to conjugal gentlemanliness. The cad."

"We ought to get under cover. It's going to rain; the cows are lying down," said Lucy restlessly.

"Oh well, even a cow is human and may err," said Emily.

But the stars became gradually absorbed in darkness.

As the final darkness fell they came to a deserted village consisting of a roadhouse, a shack or two and a barn, all empty. The travellers had with them dill pickles, a cucumber, canned tomatoes, raw eggs, raw potatoes and soda-crackers. They had also accumulated various bottles, one of very fulsome country-saloon port wine, two of gin, one of vermouth and two of whiskey.

The meal, eaten seated on the bare floor of the old roadhouse, seemed blessed. There was so much to drink. They all felt as if they had left themselves gloriously behind. There was no hint of life in the village except — far off — the asthmatic and difficult cry of a donkey. And a dog strayed in and joined the travellers. It did not seem to mind the fact that they all tried to be funny at its expense. Tam pulled its tail, lifted it up by its tail.

"The way to flatter a dog," said Emily, "is to say, 'What a nice new tail you are wearing today, darling.' Dogs are frightfully sensitive about criticism of their tails. Of course most dogs have only one tail which they wear weekdays and Sundays, but they would never admit that. They only think to themselves, 'How lucky I chose this one—I hesitated between the one with the black pin-spot and the plain white one—and how lucky it still looks new."

"That reminds me of my new puce stockings," said Melsie Ponting. "Do you know that no less than three gentlemen acquaintances—old beaux of mine, you know—stopped me on Geary to say how cute they looked. Don't you want to say something about my puce stockings, Banner?"

Emily whispered incautiously to Edward, "I think she even sleeps with mistletoe over her bed."

Edward was strongly stroking the dog's head. "The point of a dog," he said, "is that you can always pretend to yourself that the dog is saying to itself, 'Well say, this is a feller worth knowing.' They always look like that. No dog ever will show that he despises you."

"Edward," said Emily, "are your spirits always at half mast?"

Edward had an acute pain in his head, under his eyebrow. But his mind seemed to him detached from the pain and extraordinarily facile. He could hear well, he felt, but this was because Banner Hope was singing in such a sharp voice. Edward said, "It is more dramatic to be sad than to be happy, anyway, Emily. Everything that is meant to be dramatic is sad. The song that Hope is singing is— like all jazz songs—about being far away from where you want to be."

"Sadness is too easy," said Emily. "It is like mother-love and the weakness of little children and the old home and the maiden's prayer—a too easy short cut to drama. All my life I have been dramatic but I have never arrived at drama by sadness."

There seemed to be things rolling about under Edward's forehead. He thought they were loaded dice; they did not feel like balls, they hurt too much and had too many corners. He was almost pleased when he tried to stand and found himself too giddy.

Edward realised for the first time that it was raining outside. There were miles of air full of rain, like steel bars between him and safe towns and a warm bed.

"Gee!" exclaimed Melsie, unremittingly facetious. "Edward's British standards have fallen down on him. One twist too many in the lemon peel, Mr. Williams."

But Rhoda saw his eyes and rose with that tolerant yet exasperated look to which Edward was accustomed when he needed sympathy. There was wild agony in his forehead. He fell down. He rolled upon one side and then on the other. For a second he saw Emily looking detached, looking at him with an expression of excited contempt. Was she saying, "Oh, what a party!" to herself? Rhoda pressed her hands firmly over his eyes, her cold hands moved firmly about his forehead. . . .

Edward was not good at bearing pain although he was fairly well accustomed to the exercise. It was only after disgracing himself in his own eyes and in Emily's several times by crying in the car that he found himself in a ward in a San Francisco hospital.

It was immediately apparent that he could not escape an operation. The surgeon tapped his forehead impressively and his gold teeth gleamed briskly down upon the horizontal Edward.

"I wouldn't carry those sinuses about with me, my friend, not in that condition, not for half of John D. Rockefeller's pile."

Edward would not have minded continuing to carry his sinuses about exactly as they were. He vaguely treasured his afflictions. Without them he would not have felt interesting. Once, when a palmist told him that the latter part of his life would be spent in perfect health, Edward was definitely disappointed. However, an operation had its dramatic side, at least in anticipation and in retrospect. At the time it was a humiliation and a terror.

"General anæsthetic absolutely unnecessary," the

gold-mouthed surgeon had said. "It's as simple as letting off a gun. I'll take out your tonsils at the same time. You won't know a thing about it. You'll be out batting with your friends in three days."

Early one morning a man in white helped the pale Edward on to a white-sheeted vehicle which ran quickly on white and furtive castors. There was no pillow on the vehicle, and Edward, perfectly horizontal, darting head first along strange smelling corridors, felt like a torpedo whizzing towards destruction. "As simple as letting off a gun."

The surgeon, waiting in a sort of loose-box furnished in white, was dressed in white. His manner had lost the affability which had hitherto characterised it. Even his gold teeth were hidden by a white mask which, like the mask of a Turkish woman, hid the lower part of his face. He further obscured his face by covering one eye with a saucer made of mirror. The pupil of his eye could be seen through a hole in the middle of the saucer, restless and malevolent like a spider in its web. Edward was draped in gauze by a nurse. The smell of drugs and disinfectants was so strong that it seemed as if the walls must burst.

There was now no escaping from what the surgeon was going to do. The only thing one could do was to hinder him in his work.

"Keep still, keep still . . ." said the surgeon in a harsh voice. "Stop that noise, you fool."

THE POOR MAN

Edward was afraid and he intended to stop the noise but he heard his own voice still bursting from his lungs. "Ah-ow. ·. . ah-ow. . ."

He wished to implore the surgeon to stop and let him rest from pain and the feeling of ubiquitous blood, but the cocaine in his throat prevented him from articulating. Every time the surgeon struck his terrible little chisel, Edward winced violently. He was very anxious that the surgeon should realise how unusually sensitive he was. He wanted the surgeon to be sorry for him. But the surgeon was angry. He tapped Edward's forehead with barely suppressed anger. "I'm within a third of an inch of your brain here," he said. "It's up to you whether I can put this bit of work through or not."

Edward writhed. The nurse took his hand. "She's sorry," thought Edward.

There was blood everywhere. Some blood on the white apron that was stretched across the surgeon's stomach. Sweat was falling from the surgeon's chin.

"Take him away," said the surgeon suddenly and loudly. It was over. Full of shame because of his forlorn and hideous condition, Edward was wheeled quickly along the corridors. A man on crutches in a check woollen dressing-gown stared at his outraged and disordered face. Edward made feeble movements with his hands and the nurse covered his face with part of the sheet. "Now people will think I am dead. They will get quite a thrill," thought Edward and lay very still. When they took the sheet away he was beside his bed in the long bleak ward. All the other patients were looking greedily at him. Edward wanted to tell the nurse of his horror and discomfort but the cocaine still blocked his utterance. He could not mould his voice into syllables.

He hoped intensely that Emily would not come to see him while he was padded with bloodstained cotton-wool. He made up little tests to find out whether she would come. "If the sunlight reaches the chin of the man opposite before a tram goes by outside I shall know that she will not come until I am really fit to let her see me."

In answer to a croak from the man opposite, the nurse came and pulled the blind down with a peevish flounce. Most of the nurses in that ward visited on everyone who made a request the irritation they had accumulated by reason of scores of other requests. If Edward asked for anything he was made to feel as if he had asked for the same thing an unreasonable number of times. Only when the doctors were there the nurses spoke in soft optimistic voices and patted the patients' shoulders genially and called them "This poor boy. . . ."

Edward's test was spoilt by the pulling down of the blind. He betted with himself on whether the facetious man with bristly hair would ring the bell for the nurse before the blind man next to him did so. The facetious man called the nurses, "Say, Sad-

die," and asked them about their beaux. No nurse
was ever irritable with him. Sometimes he rang the
bell specially to tell the nurse that he was so hollow
he could put himself outside a whole steer, and the
nurses, though they gave him nothing, never seemed
to be annoyed by his cheerful importunity.

Edward thought that no-one in the world cared
that he was ill. He did not want Emily to come
and see him in his undignified condition. But he
would have liked her to come to the door of the
ward with a great splendid tangle of salmon-colored
roses and be stopped there by a grave sweetfaced
nurse, who would tell her that Mr. Williams was too
seriously ill to see anyone. Then Emily would ask,
"Is there any danger?" in an anxious voice that he
had never heard, and the nurse would shake her
grave sweet head and say, "One never knows. He is
suffering terribly. The surgeon had to operate
within a third of an inch of his brain." Edward fell
into a half sleep imagining the roses that Emily
would bring and lay against his lips.

When he awoke he saw Banner Hope walking
away from him towards the door of the ward.

"Hey!" said Edward in a thick desperate voice.
A week before he would have refused to believe
that the sight of Banner Hope could ever give him
pleasure.

"Why, why, why . . ." said Mr. Hope, turning
round guiltily. Edward saw at once that the visitor
had been glad to find the patient asleep. It had

been to Mr. Hope an opportunity to acquire merit as a benevolent friend without the effort of expressing benevolence. "Why, why, why . . . isn't this just too bad? . . ."

He looked inquisitively at Edward's miserable face.

"Now, don't you say a thing, Edward. The nurse has told me how it is. You gotter lie low and say nothing and I'll give you noos of all the folks. All your friends surely are peeved with these old sawbones for carving you about this way. I should say so. Yes, indeed."

This unprecedented burst of sympathy at once restored to Edward a pale gleam of the melancholy heroic light in which it was his constant effort to see himself. Still the name of Emily had not yet been mentioned and he tried to point this out. But his throat still played him false.

"Eb-gy . . ."

"That's all right. That's all right. I get you perfectly. You gotter let uncle do all the tongue work. Let me see now. . . . Well, there's Melsie Stone Ponting. She's a sport now. . . . What d'you guess she said when she knew you were sick? Why, she said—well, mebbe I'd better not tell you after all. . . . Anyway it was very smart and showed how crazy she was about you. Avery Bird I haven't seen recently, he naturally can't think of a thing except Rhoda's indictment. I guess you've heard how Rhoda was arrested the day we all got

home from Yosemite. Indicted for what they call
Criminal Syndicalism. Some of the dope she put
across at the W. I. L. A. kinda got somebody's
goat. You know, when we'd left you at the hospital
some of us went round for a drink at Rhoda's studio.
There's a kind of an old she-janitor, you know,
located in the basement, and she met us and said how
the cops had been and opened Rhoda's bureau and
gotten a wad of papers out of it. Rhoda surely
was mad, and Avery—who almost never lets up on
his detached pose or says anything except epigrams
—I'll say he blasphemed quite a bit. And right
there in the middle of that little tableau two plain-
clothes cops walked in. The door was still open
and they walked in and there was Rhoda up to her
elbows in her bureau, trying to find out which papers
they'd gotten hold of. Well, it was a fair cinch.
There was no getting around it. One of the cops
read the warrant; it was all about sabbotidge and
advocating unlawful methods of effecting political
changes. They seemed to know a whole heap about
sister Rhoda. She didn't answer back any. She
smiled and looked white. Avery said a hell of a
lot, but they didn't take much account of him. They
took all our names and addresses. Of course, it's
a long ways from indictment to conviction. Avery
says he's not taking much on her chances, she's got
in good and deep. The 'What Is Liberty' offered to
put up her bail money—but Rhoda's got plenty of
dough herself. For some reason she isn't accepting

bail. It seems like if she's got to be arrested she wants to have it done thorough. She's always been crazy about prisoners and jails. . . ."

"Ebb-ly . . ." hiccoughed Edward.

The nurse was beckoning to Banner. The sedate wives and mothers of other patients followed by their scrubbed and creaking children were willingly submitting to authority and leaving the ward.

"Say, I must be moving along," said Banner Hope with alacrity. "What's that you say? Emily? Oh, Emily's gone to China. Take care of yourself, Edward, some of your friends'll be around again some time soon. . . ."

Edward was left in such an unrelieved condition of depression that he was on the verge of peace. "Gone to China . . . Gone to China . . . Gone to China . . ." his mind chanted to itself to the rhythm of the pulse drumming in his ears. He reminded himself without ceasing that Emily had gone to China. To do so put the finishing touch to his orgy of despair. But all the time he felt certain that his ears had really played him false. All the time a little secret unadmitted factory in his mind was circulating hope by making phrases with similar vowel sounds. "He must have said, 'Emily's doing fine,' or he must have said, 'Emily's reading Heine,' or he must have said, 'Emily—how do *I* know?'" The rhymes became less and less probable as Edward approached sleep. "Penny-a-liner . . . Asia Minor . . . Clementina . . . Norah Criner . . ."

But gone to China seemed the most absurd of all.

Edward was long enough in this hospital to fit a kind of bare innocent interlude into his experience. No other visitor came to see him during the three weeks of his illness, and he had leisure to build upon the dark and sordid foundation of his life a sort of airy trivial superstructure of interests. He watched the manners of the nurses. He became interested in human temperatures, weights, symptoms and face-tious gossip connected with physical details. The watch under his pillow became his most intimate friend and guide. Waking up at six o'clock, bathing, and bed-making were an intolerable nuisance, but he was much concerned if the nurses were a moment late. The whole day was enlivened by the jokes or scoldings of the nurses. A new joke was hardly ever made in the ward, but the old ones were always suc-cessful. All the men laughed at them because they were glad that the temper of the nurses made joking possible. Sometimes the doctors were late and, though no-one loved the doctors, everyone was exas-perated with them for being late. Sometimes the doctors were so late that the breakfasts became tired of waiting, and then all the patients ate their break-fasts with a sense of incompleteness and danger. Meals were very important. Sometimes there were little red jellies at the midday meal, and when the cheerful glitter of these jellies blossomed on all the approaching trays Edward was full of an almost gay anticipation. There were no books to read, only magazines. To the nurses a magazine was a book. Any magazine would do. One did not mention the titles of books or magazines in the ward; one asked for "a book to read" as one would ask for a glass of milk. Edward was called by doctors and nurses "a great student" because he was always reading a magazine. He was not critical enough to refuse to read the bad literature that was placed before him. Sometimes he quite enjoyed the sentimental love stories. He read the comic pages with a somber interest. And he often made little tunes in his head to fit the poems, most of which seemed to have been written in imitation of each other. Some of the poems were patriotic and these annoyed Edward; it seemed so silly that anyone should love any country but England to the point of writing bad rhymes in its honor. Edward's mind was tired, too tired to feel very acutely the need of better fare. Others in the ward were more conscious than he. The man next to Edward liked the works of Gene Stratton Porter; he thought the tales of this writer very moral and very deep. He often told their plots in great detail to Edward, announcing himself as "considerable of a student like yourself." This man, who had a thin voice all on one note, was fond of talking to his neighbors at night. He would say, "Hope I'm not disturbing you folks," and nobody dared to say, "You are." They were all rather gentlemanly and talked a good deal about Americanism and the ad-

vantages of American education. In health they
frequented movies rather than saloons. They all
had wives or very respectable sweethearts who came
conscientiously to sit with them during visiting hours.
You could distinguish the sweethearts from the wives
by their habit of bringing tight bundles of flowers
and flinging them down ungraciously on the stomachs
of the afflicted. Wives never did this. The wives
brought snorting and bubbling babies instead of
flowers. Neither wives nor sweethearts had anything much to say. They all looked as if they took
for granted that the invalids were going to die.
Visiting the sick seemed to embarrass them hope-
lessly.

Visiting hours were always exciting to Edward
because Emily might come. He still boasted to himself that she had gone to China and that he was sunk
in despair, but actually he felt convinced that he had
mistaken Banner Hope's meaning. When he should
next see her he would tell her of his mistake as a
sort of heroically tragic joke. She would come any
day now and sit beside his bed and tears would come
into his eyes and his thin hand would grope for hers
and for a moment they would both be unable to
speak. Then he would say simply, "They told me
you had gone." And she would think, "Could I
ever find a more faithful lover than this?" and she
would touch his hot thin cheek with her cold fingers.

He hated the nights. Either he would stay awake
and watch the dim sickly light upon the ceiling and

think of his dreary yet too expensive room at the hotel absorbing money all this time, and think of the senseless and exasperating death of Jimmy at Loos, and think of money again and of the fact that he could not get his complexion clear—directly one set of spots healed another began. Or else he would sleep and dream cruelly and grotesquely of endless arid journeys and of beautiful anticipations that withered away and of missing trains—never of Emily.

In the daytime he would forget the hateful night. All day till about six, when the night clamored to be remembered, he was almost contented.

CHAPTER FIVE

Close akin my warriors are;
From the humming bird that swings
All a-quiver, like a star
In a radiance of quick wings—
—To the tiger mountains, stricken
  Into stillness by a breaking
  Curse. Behold, they stir and quicken,
  Gods shall tremble at their waking. . . .
Lo, my warriors, close akin,
An impregnable alliance.
  Drop thy sword and thy defiance,
  Bow thy head and let them in.

To EMERGE from this mild life was like falling
into the sea from a safe deck. Edward found himself suddenly in his dark viewless room at the hotel.
He could not find anyone who could tell him where
Emily was. He could hardly walk. The ground
seemed strangely near when he walked. He managed to go to Rhoda's studio. It was empty. The
janitor could only say with some pride, "Mrs. Bird
has gotten herself jailed. . . ."

Nothing seemed left to Edward but San Francisco
itself. Nothing was left that he could grasp; his
personal hold on the happy city had disappeared.

He felt as if he held a cold hard diamond in his hand. A diamond on the palm of the hand has no value, no value until another hand touches it or eyes desire it, or until it is set in a crown.

All his days Edward sat alone with an aching head either in his room or in the lobby of the hotel. In the lobby he sat in the midst of overdressed painted women waiting for their beaux. They were all hostile to him and to one another. In revenge he dwelt on the fact that their hair, waved and padded under light nets, looked like wigs and that, though they looked angrily at one another, they all tried to look alike. Sometimes one of them would have an "adventure"; a strange stray beau would find a pretext to get into conversation and they would talk impertinently and with heavy facetiousness for a time.

Edward sat morbidly rejoicing that he was as much different from them as it was possible to be. He even valued the pain in his head because it set him apart from them.

One day a familiar face among the waiting women occurred like one of the dreams that he could not believe in. It was Mrs. Melsie Ponting but Edward ran to her like a lover. She quite obviously regretted his appearance; obviously she did not wish him to know whom she intended to meet there. She enjoyed the excitement of concealing something. She had a rendezvous with the medical student, Pike, whose face Edward had neither liked nor committed to memory. The danger of discovery by Edward, therefore, was very slight, but Mrs. Ponting fortunately did not know this. She loved petty danger connected with petty love. The excitement made her eyes look almost as large as they were painted.

Edward leaned towards her eagerly and asked her for news of all his friends except Emily.

"My dear, isn't it exciting about Rhoda!" chattered Melsie. "I'm perfectly sure she'll get the maximum sentence. She's so high and mighty she doesn't have any of the artifices that you and me would probably get away with. She won't even come out of jail on bail. Avery Bird is mad. Everybody wants to find Avery to ask him for news, but he's like a spook—you never find him unless you're not looking for him, and then you see him speeding in a taxi down Van Ness towards the Hall of Justice. My dear, I must tell you a joke on Banner Hope—you know he is located in Oakland, but he doesn't like to have us know it—who would? Banner vamped a flapper at Jove Pinelli's and took her —where d'you think?—to Rhoda's empty studio. This is how he squared the janitor——"

"Melsie, tell me, where is Emily?"

Melsie was affronted. She was glad that she had something to say that would hurt Edward.

"Emily? Oh, Emily's gone to China."

Edward was at once very angry. He was so angry that there was a swollen feeling below his ears. It was outrageous that mention of the innocent and lovely name of Emily should produce nothing but this shocking parrot cry—"Emily? Oh, Emily's gone to China. . . ." Why was this conspiracy directed against him? Emily would not wish it. Emily would wish gentle and exciting things to be said of her. . . . "Emily is here—on her way to see you. . . ." "Emily is gathering poppies for you in the fields behind Alameda. . . ." "Emily would never go far from you, Edward. . . ."

"No, she is shameless. That is the message she meant to leave for me. "Emily? Oh, Emily's gone to China."

"Yes, sirree—bob, she's gone to China," repeated Melsie. "Furthermore, Edward, she's taken my kiddie with her. It was a bully chance for me, since you were such a piker. They're all touring the Orient together—she and my honey and Mr. and Mrs. McTab."

Mrs. Ponting lived entirely from her own point of view. This was her life, to charm those whom she needed, to wound those who rebuffed her, to ignore those with whom she was not acquainted. Her imagination was completely blind and deaf; wounds or joys outside of herself were inconceivable to her. She was glad of her present advantage over Edward, the advantage of the wounder over the wounded. There was nothing deliberate in her gladness; simply she did not know pain unless she felt it.

Edward had very little money. His operation
and the hospital had absorbed almost all that he
had. He owed the rest—and more—to his hotel.
He had no shame about accepting money. He lacked
manly pride. If Melsie Ponting had offered him
money he would have taken it gladly. He would
have pretended to himself that it was a great struggle and a great humiliation to accept money but
really he would have been delighted. He had never
had any understanding of money, no apprehension
of poverty, no skill in keeping money, no anticipation of increasing it. The etiquette and decencies
of money made no appeal to him. It is hardly
necessary to add that Mrs. Ponting did not offer
him money, even when she had asked him, "Well,
for goodness' sake, Edward, why don't you go to
the Orient too as you planned?" and Edward had
replied, "I haven't any money."

One thing Edward was not too proud but too shy
to do. He could not actually ask for money. San
Francisco is full of generous people; almost any of
the guests at his party would have helped him. But
he did not know how he would introduce the subject. There was no equality of friendship where
Edward was concerned.

Rhoda Romero had offered to pay him to go to
China. "Did she know Emily was going? No, she
wanted to get rid of me. I am a weariness to
Rhoda. She was trying to mislay me kindly. And
now I have mislaid Emily."

Every day for a week after that Edward walked about on Van Ness Avenue in the hope of seeing Avery Bird speeding past in a taxi. Edward thought he would throw himself in front of the taxi. For the first time Avery Bird, now in trouble himself, would look gently on Edward. Van Ness Avenue is the Bond Street of motor cars. I have no doubt that little homely Fords, bragging in the public garages at night, talk about the latest fashions in windshields on Van Ness. Van Ness also leads to the Hall of Justice. Edward moved from window to window examining the shining new automobiles and constantly turning sharply, expecting to see Rhoda, restored to freedom, coming to meet him.

Once he went to the Hall of Justice to ask if he might speak to Rhoda. His appearance seemed to irritate the public servants whom he addressed. They offered him no assistance. He wrote a long and introspective letter to Rhoda, care of the City Jail, but he received no answer.

He was a little stronger in health and felt capable of filling almost any position except those which were advertised in the papers. Finally he was obliged to apply for a job as salesman for a patent egg-beater. But he was told that he lacked punch. He became desperate and attempted to become a grocer's assistant in a poor part of the city. The boss, a bustling Greek, said he didn't want no white-collar guys. Then Edward called at the office of a company that seemed inexplicably anxious that young

America should become acquainted with the works of Milton. To this end they had printed a *Milton for Our Boys*. It was not, of course, "in poetry." Poetry is unhealthy for children, unmanly for Our Boys. On the contrary, this was Milton's genius made clear for immature minds, as the Jewish, violet-powdered young lady in the office cleverly recited by heart to Edward. The advertisement had demanded the services of highminded young men and women of college education interested in public service, so Edward rightly felt that his tendency to white-collarism would be no disadvantage here. A college education, it appeared, was, in most cases, necessary to enable the public-spirited young men and women to persuade the hardfisted mothers of Our Boys not only to pay one dollar down and procure a five dollar *Paradise Lost* in their homes, but in addition, to sign a form ordering four more works of Milton—*Paradise Regained for Our Boys, Collected Works of Milton for Our Boys One, Collected Works of Milton for Our Boys Two* and *Milton and America* by Spilwell G. Mundt. Any enlightened mother who should commit herself to the purchase of the whole series would be presented, absolutely free, with a beautiful picture of George Washington standing under the Stars and Stripes looking flushed and repressed as though he were suffering from indigestion. It was probably felt by the firm that this gift would gloss over the fact that, unfortunately, the immortal writer to be introduced to Our Boys was not, strictly speaking, a hundred per cent American.

The fact that Edward was English appealed to the Jewish young lady in charge as rather piquant. It seemed to her that his speech—though, of course, ridiculously foreign—was somehow "cultured." She therefore waived the fact that he could not claim a college education. She gave him a little pamphlet showing him what to say to the mothers of North Berkeley. The pamphlet opened with advice about persistence—never get discouraged—go right on ringing till somebody comes—if possible step inside the door as soon as it is opened—be cheery and sympathetic—never take the first No for an answer, nor the second either; many firstrate deals have been put through after two or three refusals—remember it's mother's job to grip the pocketbook tight, but—well, she's only a woman after all, and doesn't she want to see that little scamp of hers grow up into a big, wise, cultured woman? The opening sentence of the attack was, "Say, Mother, what are you doing for your boy?" But a few comments on the weather or the view—any cheery topic that presented itself—to be inserted before that opening sentence, were in order. Edward would receive ten per cent commission—fifty cents for each work of Milton sold. "Some of our men make five to seven dollars a day," said the young lady in an inspiring voice. "And North Berkeley's a clean field . . ."

THE POOR MAN

On asking what a clean field meant, Edward was told that—so far as the Company knew—no other highminded young men or women had tried to induce the mothers of North Berkeley to buy Milton. Edward was glad of this. He could imagine that a busy mother called repeatedly to the door to show reason why she should not buy Milton for her boy would in time become difficult to deal with.

Five dollars a day was thirty dollars a week. He could live on two dollars a day and save half his earnings. On a hundred and fifty dollars he thought he could get to China. He could save a hundred and fifty dollars in ten weeks.

He was not often so full of hope.

First he went out with another public-spirited young man by whose skill he was supposed to learn and benefit. This young man had facetious and astonished eyes, a fat, ingrowing nose, and tight high-waisted clothes which proved him to have had the Western equivalent of a college education.

Edward was much impressed by his methods. The first house they invaded was a lonely eccentric house crouching behind a thin mask of young eucalyptus trees. In the garden a Japanese was working, and from him Edward's instructor ascertained that the mistress of the house was not at home and that even if she had been at home she would have been found to be childless. Undaunted by this, the instructor, followed by the surprised Edward, ran towards the house holding out eager hands towards a female "help" who was shaking a mat out of the garden door.

"Has she gone? Have I missed her?" wailed the instructor in a poignant voice.

"Do you mean Mrs. Watson?" asked the credulous help sympathetically. "Yes . . . Why, isn't that just too bad! She went out on a errand. She'll be right back, I guess. Don't you want to come in and wait?"

"I'll say I do," said the instructor, rubbing his hands together and hissing inwards through his teeth in the manner of a real family friend. He went into the living room. "Gee, it's good to be here again."

The reply of the admiring help was an offer of drinks for him and Edward.

With a glass of light beer in his hand the instructor walked about looking at the books on the shelves. "Kipling . . . Lawrence . . . Hergesheimer . . . Hardy . . . aw shucks! Say, ma'am, you interested in classical litera*ture?"*

Edward, who hated beer, was not happy. The situation seemed to him only evanescently comfortable. Besides, the opening—Say mother, what are you doing for your boy?—was plainly ruled out here.

"I'll say I am," replied the help. "That is to say—I'm not one of these highbrows, but I get a lot of kick out of a good tale."

"You've read all the British classics of course," continued the instructor. "Say listen, you know it's a fact that although these Britishers neglect their teeth and don't know the first thing about sanitation or democracy, their classic authors do surely deliver the goods. Some guys is so darn narrowminded they could pretty near meet their ears at the back of their heads, but I say hand over credit where credit is due. You know any of the dope by this guy they call John Milton?"

"Does he write for the movies?"

"May have done, for all me," replied the instructor cautiously. "Anyway, he's dead now. But his tales certainly are red-meat tales. I'll ask you to give these books the once over—John Milton put into good peppy American prose and il*lus*trated by one of the swellest artists in Kansas city."

The help at last became suspicious. "What you carrying those books around for?" she asked. "You one of these fresh agent nuts? I thought you said you was a friend of Mrs. Watson."

"I'm a friend of everyone that's got a taste for classical litera*ture*," replied the instructor courageously. "I'm a public benefactor. I tell you I'm ready to put into your hands this minute this illustrated Milton Dee Lux for one dollar down. It's a unique opportunity——"

"Now you can just quit right away," shouted the help, snatching up her O-Cedar mop with a threatening gesture. "You got no business to of came.

125

Ef Mrs. Winton S. Watson was to come into this room and find a coupla two-cent drummers drinking her beer—well, good-night. No, I won't hear another word, you can just get busy moving, the quicker the better."

Edward led the retreat. The instructor made a heroic stand and Edward, trembling in the garden, heard a sort of duet proceeding from the living room for a few seconds. Then the instructor, humming brazenly, joined him.

"That dame certainly was a goatgetter," he admitted. "These folks is fifty fifty. Sometimes they fall for dope like that most before you begin putting it over. Sometimes they don't, that's all there is to it. It's fifty fifty."

Mathematically speaking he was wrong. The percentage of weak housewives willing to invest money in the Classics was nothing like fifty per cent. Yet the general result of the day was not discouraging to Edward. He looked back with a certain excitement to a day spent climbing up steep geranium-bordered steps to inexplicably friendly interviews. He looked forward still to making five dollars a day and refused to analyse, even to himself, the differences of manner between himself and his instructor.

Next day he was allowed to go by himself.

He studied North Berkeley on the map like a lover studying the portrait of his mistress. He decided to begin work at a street the name of which reminded him, without reason, of Emily. He made the stopping of the street-car a secret test of the coming day's chance of success. If it should stop at his corner for passengers other than himself it would mean success—five dollars—perhaps a record —ten dollars. . . . A group of women stopped the car at his corner and he was very glad until, on calling at the first two houses, he found that the group had consisted of potential clients of Milton, departing for their marketing. At the third house the housewife was in. Edward did not begin with, "Say, mother, what are you doing for your boy?" He lost his head.

He began lamentably, "I say, I've got a book here to sell."

The mistress of the house shook her head sadly at him. "I dare say you have, but I haven't the money to spend."

"Oh, sorry . . ." said Edward and turned towards the street again.

"Wait a moment. I believe you're English. I am English too—a remittance woman. How rash of you to take up salesman's work in a country of salesmen. Would you like to come in?"

"I have my methods and the instructor had his," thought Edward complacently as he followed her in. "The results seem to be the same."

He looked with cool hope at the "remittance woman." She had rather a flat crumpled face and very soft looking matt skin. Her pince-nez were the only firm thing in her face; they obviously pinched very strongly.

"I must introduce you to my only friend," she said waving her hands towards an apparently empty corner of the living-room. Then Edward saw that a canary was suspiciously eyeing him from the dresser.

Edward chuckled doubtfully. "Have you really no other friends?" he said, telling himself that the woman was rather morbid.

"None," replied the Englishwoman placidly. "The people I know in England pay me to make my home on another continent. I am unfortunate in being hateful to everyone I meet."

"Haven't you any relations?" asked Edward lamely.

"I am not married and my sisters in England hate me. I once was determined to get married and even got so far as to wait in a white dress at a church in North London. But the man changed his mind and never came. Indeed he did not change his mind, he hated me all along. Everybody does."

Edward was overwhelmed. The woman seemed to him offensive. Did she suppose she was the only person in the world who had Known Grief? However, he felt a little proud because she was telling him these things. He thought he must have a sympathetic face—"the face of one who had been down into the depths." He drew the corners of his mouth down to make his face more sympathetic.

"When I say everybody," added the woman, "of course I am excepting Edward."

Edward dropped his sympathetic expression just as it was properly adjusted. "Excepting who?"

She waved her hand again towards the canary, which flew across on to her shoulder. "Edward," she explained. "He loves me. He loves my hair and my lips. He pecks and pulls at my hair in the mornings when I let him out of his cage. I lie in bed late—I have nothing to get up for— And Edward holds my chin between his nervous little claws and pushes his beak between my lips . . ."

Edward Williams looked with dislike at her hair and her lips. Her hair was grey and had a middle-aged, tangled curl in it. Her lips were dry and rather grey too.

"My name is Edward too," he said.

"Well," said the remittance woman, pleased. "Isn't that a nice stroke of chance? Tell me about yourself. Why are you attempting an unlikely job like this?"

Edward at once felt pity in the air. He groped for pity instinctively. He told her in a plaintive voice about his loneliness, the fact that he had no mother and that Jimmy was killed at Loos, he told her of his efforts to support himself, of his love for Emily. . . .

When he had finished he felt only slightly guilty and looked down at the book he wished her to buy. She did not want it but surely she could afford to buy something she did not want from a kindred soul. He would refuse at first her offer to buy his book, he thought.

"We are rather alike," she said. "We neither of us get on with the world."

Her voice was almost jealous. She so rarely met competition in her line.

"Yes," said Edward. "But you are more fortunate than I, if you are hated. I am ignored, which is much worse."

She assented doubtfully. "Certainly everybody hates me," she insisted. It was her one vanity and her support.

There was a pause and they looked at each other with dislike.

"I don't need your book," she said. "But I have five dollars to spare. I suppose you are insulted now. You can put the five dollars in your pocket and spare me the trouble of breaking the back of my bookshelf with such a straw as *Milton for Boys*. Take it and hate me for it if you like. I am used to that."

Edward held the flaccid money in his hand. He thought, "It pays to be pathetic." He despised himself at the same time and thought, "Even Banner Hope would be shocked at this. Why haven't I automatically evolved a proud personality like everyone else?"

She opened the door by way of dismissing him. "You will curse me whenever you think of this," she said. "It will be a satisfaction to you. People always curse those who pity them."

"I shan't," said Edward, putting the five dollar bill in his pocket. "I don't believe anyone hates you or curses you. You deceive yourself."

When he looked back from the street her affronted face was still turned towards him. With relief and irritation he decided never to think of her again.

He sold no books either that day or the next. He did not dare to use the provided formula—Say mother—. He had nothing definite to use instead. To one or two mothers who were too courteous to slam the door he murmured broken suggestions about the superiority of Milton to the movies. It was a false step. The movies, to the American middle class, are a substitute for religion. For uplift the home depends on the movies. Edward found himself guilty of blasphemy. Milton appeared in the light of a criminal heresy.

After two days Edward went, like Noah's homing dove, to the office, Milton still in his beak.

"There's something wrong with the district," he complained to the young lady there. "The word book seems to mean nothing to them. All the artistic words have changed their meaning in California. *Book* means magazine, *Music* means jazz, *Act* means behaving, *Picture* means a snapshot. They haven't even a place to keep books. They have nothing but old *Ladies' Home Journals* on their dressers."

Edward thought of *Milton for Our Boys* now as a valuable but wronged book.

The young woman naturally did not pay much attention to what he was saying. But she came from Calistoga and was excited to meet so rare a specimen as an educated foreigner. She was, in mind, face and fashion, a typical young woman of the Wild West. She had no interest or recreation whatever, apart from flirtation. Englishmen were all nearly lords in her democratic imagination. They were therefore laughable but worth charming. She had just mislaid her last steady beau so she was at the moment a little susceptible. She had, temporarily, no special man in mind when powdering her nose to an amethyst color or corrugating her dark, dull, padded hair.

"Why, isn't that just too bad?" she said arching her false looking eyebrows caressingly at Edward. "Well, say, listen, don't you want to try out Napa County and Sonoma County? One of our men is crazy to have us send someone there; he says there's a lot doing out that ways. My own home-city, Calistoga, is some cultured burg, let me tell you. My brother made fifteen dollars once in his vacation, boosting the *Saturday Evening Post*. Say, I go home sometimes over the week end. If you fix up to work that locality, don't you want to call in at our place? I'd love to have you meet my Mom."

She was planning to say to her Mom, "Say Mom, I've got a new steady, an English lord."

132

"Are there azaleas in those parts? And does the company pay one's fare?" asked Edward.

The young lady looked uncomfortable and paused. "Say Steve, I guess I would better put you wise on something. This firm doesn't do much of the faith, hope and charity turn to folks in their country lines. They only come across with your trolley fare on commission—same as in Berkeley. No sales—no cash. I don't say I get much kick out of the way they act, but there they are. But see here, my Pop's coming down to Berkeley to gimme a ride home next Saturday in our old Dodge. Don't you want to come along? And when we get to our place, brother'll loan you his wheel, seeing you're a friend of mine. I've got a hunch, Steve, that you're not one of these way-up born-to-the-manner drummers. Don't you find it hard to impress strangers? I thought so. Us up-and-coming Californians, you know, you can't get in with us without you've got a lot of punch. Europeans don't have any punch, the way I figure it. Well, we can't all be born where we want, can we?"

Edward was pleased to have excited sympathy in one more breast. "Our hero has that indefinable *something* that only women's subtler sensibilities can appreciate. . . ."

He persisted in his fruitless missionary efforts among the mothers of North Berkeley until the following Saturday. At a given time he proceeded to a given rendezvous in Oakland to meet his patroness—whose name was Mame Weber—and her Pop and her brother Cliff.

Cheek by jowl with Miss Weber he bounced upon the back seat of Pop's Dodge car. "Better if you'd put your arm where it oughter be," advised Miss Weber, indicating her own ribs. "Only mind and don't get fresh. Pop's awful strict. Say, got any candies?"

Edward looked at her blankly.

"Not even a sticka gum? Why, I'll say you're a nice beau. I'd a feller name of Al who couldn't never hardly hug me right away—his pockets was so fulla candies. Say, Ed, you got a lot to learn."

Edward accepted his rôle with surprise and pleasure. Miss Weber was of the shrinking and protectible type when motoring and, whenever the car, driven by rash brother Cliff, seemed unlikely to avoid disaster, Edward enjoyed feeling against his arm the stiffening and trembling of her thinly clothed body.

"Emily doesn't know me yet," he thought. "She has never let me show her my fine or strong side." Miss Weber took an insignificant but pleasing part in the ranks of his sensations.

Napa Valley, like an inverted rainbow, lay before him. The strange, creased, silken bodies of the hills lay behind the glassy white veil of the air. The shadows striped and varied them, and the night-green patches of oaks, beaten almost as flat as the shadows, were crammed into the canyons. On every side, at a lower and more human level, a conventional pattern of vineyards and steepled masses of bleak eucalyptus trees was printed on the valley. The orchards were alight with the bright golden green that follows the blossom season and in their shade the grass was passionately green.

> The sweet skeletons
> Of orchards fire delight.
> They fire into my sight
> Quick rays of green and bronze.
> I am pierced—I cannot bear
> Their wounding—I surrender . . .
>   The almond blossom's tender
>   Pale smoke is on the air. . . .

As the car passed quickly the ends of the aisles between the rows of delicate and jointed fruit-trees, successive rays of violent green flashed along the perspectives into Edward's eyes. Blinking at this, he hardly knew when first the mountain, Saint Helena, parted the little near hills and inserted between them its thickly blue peak.

"Hands praying . . . or steeples . . . or the peaks of mountains," thought Edward. "They are all praising God always, whether there is a God or not."

The father of Miss Weber was a retail merchant in Calistoga. He called his house not a house but a "home." "My Pop has one elegant home right in the classy part of the city of Calistoga," said Miss Weber.

THE POOR MAN

The American of the Weber type chooses many of his words for their potential catch in the throat, as it were. *Motherhood, manhood, lovelight, grip-o'-the-hand,* the movies have made words of this kind music in the American ear. But words with home in them are the most popular—*homestead, home-land, home-site, home-town, home-builder* . . . We who can live in houses and can see the word Mother in print with dry eyes or hear the glugging of some-one else's baby over its food in a cafeteria without vicarious domestic ecstasy, must seem very coarse to Americans. However, the missionary movies are with us now. We shall all no doubt eventually suffer a change of heart.

The Weber Home was made of wood, painted mustard yellow picked out in sky blue. It had a fancy roof and a jocose little castellated turret over one window, like a drunkard's hat on one side.

Mrs. Weber was not so classy as her son, her daughter and her Home. She spent much of her time in the kitchen and was at first realised by Edward only as a shrill voice calling, "Walk right in, Son, make yessell at home," in reply to her daughter's announcement, "Oh, mom, meet my new beau, Ed Williams."

Mrs. Weber, when seen as well as heard, proved to be extremely fat, though sprightly. She was powdered just as lavishly as was her daughter, but in a softer shade of mauve. She had fine dark myopic eyes; her thick black brows met and dipped under the bridge of her pince-nez. Her bosom was too enormous to seem even motherly. She had a screaming laugh which was probably one of the charms that had won her Mr. Weber and an elegant home, for she laughed most assiduously during and between jokes.

"Cheery ole dame is Mom, isn't that right, Ed?" said Miss Weber, throwing one of her pretty arms half way round the vast shoulders of her Mom.

It was a simple home. Pop might well be proud of it. He shewed, however, no signs of pride—no signs, in fact, of anything. He did not speak more than once or twice a day. Even at meals he sat half turned from the table with musing eyes fixed on one square of the carpet. He had a wrinkled thin neck like a tortoise's. His face was wrinkled and full of grievances. He explored the inside of his cheeks almost constantly with his tongue and sometimes with his finger. Often he assisted his tongue and finger by picking his teeth with any implement that came handy. His one conversation with Edward ran thus:

"Well, young feller, how much better d'you like this country than yer own?"

"No better," replied Edward nervously. He hastened to add apologetically, "You see, I have an affection for England because it's my home—I mean my homeland, as it were. Just the same as you'd like America best even if you came to England——"

Mr. Weber laughed and set his toothpick to work

on rather an inaccessible tooth. "Reckon I shouldn't think anything of England," he said in a final voice.

"Well, that's what I mean," said Edward, growing rather red. "That's rather what I feel about America, when you compare it with England."

Pop leaned forward and leveled his toothpick at Edward's face. "Now, see here, son," he said, showing only two of his left hand teeth.

Miss Weber shrieked, "Aw cut it out, Pop, and you forget it too, Ed. Pop's a reg'lar whizz at politics."

Young brother Cliff was a child of nature, a child, as it were, of urban nature. He had no reticences, it seemed to Edward, who was much afraid of him. There was no telling what young brother Cliff would say next. " 'S'matter with Ed's chin—'s'all pimples?" he would say after a long rude silence. Or, "Say Mom, Ed sweats at night same as Will useter." Edward slept in Cliff's room during the two nights of his visit. Young Cliff wore "Jazz clothes"; they were very tight under the arms. It seemed as if his clothes were made to be worn with the elbows always up, on a desk or on a lunch counter. They were very urban clothes. But Cliff was much pleased with them. He had no country clothes or country pursuits. He was frankly amused at Edward's English clothes. "Ed's clothes fit him like the shell of a peanut." Cliff's one Calistoga amusement was to stand in front of the drug-store while the Calistoga young women turned this way and that as they preened themselves on the side-walk before him.

On Sunday morning Edward accompanied Cliff on this exercise. After looking with rude intensity at the figures and legs of all the young women in sight, Cliff selected two—the two with the barest necks and the largest imitation pearls—and offered to buy them sodas. Edward and Cliff and the two young women sat in a row on tall hinged stools at the drug-store counter. Cliff hardly spoke one word to the girls, though several times he jovially kicked the shin of the nearest. Apart from this he exchanged apparently amusing but incomprehensible badinage with the soda-mixer behind the counter. The girls powdered their noses and talked in indifferent low voices to each other. They did not seem to mind being excluded from manly conversation. But twice Cliff turned to them and said—of the ice cream soda—"Slips down easy, don't it, kid?" and then Edward was shocked at the instant change of their expression to an obsequiously bright admiring look.

"I thought there were more men than women in California," said Edward afterwards. "Why do these girls cringe so, anyway before they're married?"

Cliff did not give Edward much attention. "Never too many beaux for these skirts," he said. "Say, Edward, did you see the way they was tickled to death by your British pants?"

Miss Weber was naturally more attentive to Edward than were the others, but she was disappointed in him. For three hours on a perfect Sunday afternoon she sat on the couch close to Edward in the stuffy living room, but Edward did not seem to know what was expected of him. When Miss Weber said, "Say, listen, Ed, tell me about the way English girls act with their beaux." Edward actually began to do so. Usually so sensitive about the impression he was making, he was quite complacent now.

"This girl is really pathetically taken with me," he thought. He laid before her a description of a day in Epping Forest, he produced an excerpt from his childhood, he told her of a tree with enlarged and tangled roots in which his lead soldiers used to climb. Also he mentioned a young bat which he and Jimmy had found. They made a hole for it in the tree. It stayed two days.

"Jimmy was killed at Loos," he said.

"Well, isn't that too bad . . ." said Miss Weber. She paused for a decent moment before saying, "You're a nice beau, aren't you?"

"I don't suppose you really think so," said Edward, smiling placidly. "You must have had many more amusing beaux than me."

"Oh, my no," replied Miss Weber acidly. She threw her head back on the cushions so that her round neck and fine figure were seen to advantage.

Edward redeemed himself a little by taking her hand and feeling upward along her arm as if in curiosity.

"Rather a shame," thought Edward happily, "to raise her hopes like this."

"You know, I have a true love already," he said aloud.

"I'll tell the world you have," replied Miss Weber. "Haf-a-dozen, more like. In England I guess."

"In China."

"Is that right? Well, China's a long ways off," she said and placed her head a little doubtfully on his shoulder.

"That's nice," said Edward, trying secretly to pretend that the head was Emily's. It was blasphemy, for Miss Weber's crimped hair looked sticky under its dusty net. "Poor soul, poor defenceless little woman . . ." he thought a little wearily. He had never before had such advances from a virtuous young woman, but he was already thinking of himself as a heartbreaker. He was proud but he ached for Emily.

"One's life with such people is hideous," he thought suddenly. "People like me have to pretend all the time with them. Pretend to be amused . . . to be gratfeul . . . to be sprightly . . . to be in love. If one stopped pretending one would shout, 'Oh, how hideous my life is when I am with you.' Emily is easy."

"I guess you haven't gotten on to my first name," murmured Miss Weber.

"Yes I have. It's Mame," he replied with distaste.

Only once during his visit was Edward's dramatic sense aroused, and that was when he seemed to hear Mom say to a silent and ghostlike neighbor who had dropped in, "Merry, merry, merry were they, and danced with their hair in a tremble." After studying the picture thus presented to his mental retina, Edward realised that part of what she had really said was, "It's worry, worry, worry all day about dancing . . ."

That evening, when the energies of a cheap Victrola had been directed to the delivery of a song which one could tell was a comic song about Prohibition because it was sung out of tune and with a great deal of hiccoughing, Miss Weber asked her brother for the loan of his bicycle.

"What'd I loan Ed my wheel for?" asked the frank youth. "He's not *my* beau, is he?"

"Why, Cliff, you know you haven't used it yourself in months. You're not going to act mean, are you?"

The discussion lasted for about seventy minutes. It ended thus: "Why, what'd I wanter loan Ed my wheel for? He's not *my* beau. Mom, here's Sis' beau after my wheel. He'd skip with it, as likely as not. It's my wheel anyway."

"Well, then, you won't get any more music off

my Victrola. I'll lock it up, you mean thing. Mom, isn't brother the mean thing?"

"Lock it up all you want. I can live without music, I guess. I'm not one of your British high-brow lords."

Unperturbed, Mom read *Mother's Magazine*, her square florid face resting on its many chins like a shut door at the top of steps. Mr. Weber picked his teeth with clicking noises and looked at the floor as though he could see through it.

When Edward awoke on Monday morning, Cliff was gone. Miss Weber was knocking on the door. "Brother says you can have his wheel," she said through the door. "I gotter catch my train in a minute. Come down till I show you where the wheel is."

Edward felt for a moment sorry that his eyes looked so ugly immediately after he awoke. "It'll disillusion her, poor soul," he thought, putting on his overcoat. "Perhaps it's as well . . ."

"I'd better not borrow your brother's bike, thanks awfully. He didn't seem really keen for me to have it."

"Shucks," said Miss Weber guiltily. "He's crazy for you to have it. Nothing'll happen. You can't eat it, can you? Come ahead."

The last words he ever heard from Miss Weber were spoken in the garage. "My, look at your legs! Do all Britishers wear jazz suits in bed? I'll say old Cliff got a good laugh over that suit. My, a quarter of seven . . . I must hustle. By-bye, Ed, gimme a hug. Call in at the office any time."

When Edward said good-bye to his host and hostess, Mr. Weber spat in a pointed and rude way on to a spot near Edward's left foot. It hurt Edward's feelings rather.

"Somehow I don't get on with coarse people, especially in America. Few people appreciated a man of our Hero's exquisite fibre," he thought, without much conviction.

Edward had two dollars and fifty cents. He was not a very good manager but he lived on that money for three days. He did not sell a single book.

"If I were the hero of a book," he thought once, "nobody would ever believe that I had made so complete a failure of such a simple job. Never one sale. Other people in books have ups and downs in their businesses, but I have only downs—and such deep downs. I can't think what is the matter with me. It is really that Emily is a part of me that hasn't fitted on yet—the successful and splendid part. Emily and I could be a man and a woman. Without her I am not even a man."

"Never mind. I have only to wait. People never go on in such an agony of wanting without at last getting what they want."

The further away Emily went the more did Edward forget the hopelessness of his suit. He only remembered the softer aspects of Emily's face.

The roads he chose during those three days lay

often through forests. He avoided the open, wide, concrete roads. "If I can get in with the little ranches, that'll be a cleaner field. Ranch people have boys, I suppose."

The boys did not seem to want culture in the little ranches. Some of the women could hardly speak English. Their replies were given in an accent so exotic that the sense did not penetrate to Edward's faulty hearing. When he looked at their faces, however, he was generally glad he could not understand. He was not wise in his choice of "clean fields."

Bungalows infest the slopes of the Russian River, yet almost every bungalow at which Edward knocked was apparently uninhabited, except at week-ends. There was no business there—still, there was the Russian River. A rigorous red road sawed up the dark high mountains on the south bank of the river. There were trees everywhere. Young redwoods against the sky were strangely bare and lancelike. The sun made nothing of the inconsiderable branches of the trees—it made clear only their proud back-bones. There were madrones. One would expect to bend a mandrone like rubber; its stem has the apparent texture of red rubber. And bent it is, but only by great winds. Its stem and branches are red and rose-red or gold and green-gold; it glows like a pillar of jewels and precious metals. Once a year madrone opens hundreds of little windows in its scarlet and crimson tower, little green square

windows are cut in the bark, through which joy in
the heart of the madrone looks out at spring. At
those times it is as if there was, pouring from the
innumerable windows, a most gay green and gold
light into the forest—light where sunlight cannot
enter—a low, gay light in the forest shadows. But
now madrone's windows were closed, madrone was
sealed up in its smooth shadeless red towers. The
glazed grape-colored stems of manzanita haunted
the shadows below the madrones. There were
columbines with their flowers strangely balanced in
the air like stage fairies. And most of the world
in sight was pricked by pines and firs in all shades
of green, ranging from a hot, live green to a green
that had almost the sheen of a Blue Persian cat.

The Russian River, far down, ran among mauvish
tapering islands of sand. It crouched low down
beneath the feet of the hills and the trees. The
sun-dazzle upon the river dodged behind the shoulders of the hills.

Edward tried to "work" the self-conscious summer villages and the concealed and suspicious mountain hamlets. *Milton for Our Boys* seemed to be a
drug in the forest market. Talk of uplift withered
in the smell of the sea that came up the Russian
River.

Edward slept one night simply and uncomfortably
beside the prostrate bicycle under a twisted madrone
tree, on soil thick with intimate small weeds—soil
that for the first two hours was soft and seemed a

vantage point from which to sing to the stars, but
for the rest of the night was hard and infested with
ants. Stars are stark comfort at three in the
morning.

All next day he was in sunlight on the naked low
hills that follow the line of the sea. The hills were
burnt; it seemed that they had even caught something of the colour of flame. They were burnt
tawny gold and crimson. These were the naked
hills; they were done with the draperies of
spring.

Edward bicycled briskly. He felt rather ashamed
of having to move his feet in such a brisk prancing
way; he thought that he shewed the ridiculous jaunti-
ness of a toy dog.

He was approaching *The World's Egg Center*.
The hills broke out into an eruption of white hens.
Edward thought that, just as every provincial
mother looks to London, so it must be every hen's
ambition to have an egg making its début at the
World's Egg Center. Twelve miles out of the egg
metropolis suburbs of hens were already thick on
the ground.

Apart from hens, the only flowers of that bare
country seemed to be boulders, great proud purple
boulders rooted in their own clear shadows. Sometimes little wind-bent trees, like jockeys, rode the
boulders.

Edward called upon many chicken ranchers in the
hope of introducing Milton to their boys. He was

becoming desperate. He had thirty-five cents left in the world. Chickens must be an absorbing pursuit; no rancher had any time or attention for Milton.

Edward spent twenty-five cents on a very bad meal.

After sunset he crouched under a leaning rock on the slope of a hill. He slept well and in the morning found his waking eyes on fire in the glare of a solitary gold poppy, gloriously open within three inches of his face. The poppy was thickly and incredibly golden; its petals had a sheen like a little wind on sunny water and, deep within its cup, dusted with gold, was its treasure, a tiny unkempt chrysanthemum of gold with a crisp core of black.

At the next ranch visited by Edward the disorder of his clothes, after two nights under the dishevelling stars, had its effect. A man in blue jeans, carrying a bucket of grain, met Edward at the gate and said, "We found and lifted the latch of the polar star."

Edward was no fool. After a second's surprise he realised that his ears were betraying him again.

"Sorry," he said. "I didn't quite catch what you said."

"What's that?"

"I didn't hear what you said."

"You don't need to hear anything except Keep Out," said the man waving at a terse sign rooted in a whirlpool of chickens: KEEP OUT THIS

MEANS YOU. "We don't want no hoboes here."

"My name is Edward Williams," said Edward urgently. "I want you to look at——"

"If you said you was William Randolph Hearst I wouldn't give a whoop. No, sir-ree, not in them togs. 'S'plain enough, ain't it?"

Edward bicycled briskly away. He looked himself over when he was out of sight of the ranch. His clothes were creased like the cheek of a nonagenarian. *Milton for Our Boys* was an anomaly as a bait at the end of that crumpled sleeve. He would try no more. "Our Hero was never one to fly in the face of fate." He bicycled into the Chicken-City and he was so much irritated by hunger that he hoped he would run over someone and die in the attempt. All the faces on the sidewalks made him uncontrollably angry. He went into a saloon and ordered a brandy. He was so angry that his voice trembled. He would never see Emily again. He would die in the suburbs of a chicken center. He would find another gold poppy and it would pour gold into his eyes until his eyes closed. Poppies are better than pennies on dead eyes.

"Only a matter of a few days more," said the saloon keeper in a friendly voice.

"Being deaf is as bad as being haunted," thought Edward, wondering what the man had really said. "A matter of one day more," he grunted.

"No, *sir*. June thirtieth's the last day and you

don't wanta forget it. I'll say the boys'll be around that night. What gets me's how the government put it over, but—well, I should worry I guess."

"He's talking of Prohibition," Edward realised. "Well, by the end of this week I shall be prohibited anyway."

Just as the saloon keeper began another remark, Edward turned his back irritably and sat down at a table. The brandy combined rather badly with his hunger.

There was a newspaper on the table. Rhoda Romero's name was on it in tall headlines.

Acquitted.

There was a snapshot of Rhoda, with a defensive hand to her chin, walking with one foot up. ". . . Collapsed on hearing verdict . . . Miss Romero, who is in private life Mrs. Avery Bird . . . yesterday, facing a possibility of a fourteen years' sentence, not a muscle of her face (of a Grecian type) twitches . . . today, declared free . . . attack of hysterics in court . . . hides her face among hubby's vest buttons . . . refuses to disclose her plans . . . will perhaps visit relatives in the East . . . complete nervous collapse . . ."

Edward felt absolutely no joy on Rhoda's account. "It's no use pretending," he thought. "There's no room in me now for anything but me and Emily."

He was very much excited. He read the account

three or four times. He recognised the dress that Rhoda was wearing in the snapshot. He spoke to the saloon keeper again.

"This is my greatest friend in California," he said in a trembling voice, hoping that the saloon keeper would be very much interested.

"Well, what do you know about that?" said the host, taking the paper patiently. "She's a looker too, I'll say. Well, it's good hearing for you that she ain't ona these Reds. We had a Red once blaaing around in this city—wanted a hired man's strike . . ."

"Yes, isn't it funny, I even know that dress. Those little buttons are green." Edward was quite unlike himself. He was so hungry.

"Is that right? You bin going with her, I guess," said the saloon keeper, looking at him sharply. "Well, who's to blame you, she surely looks a classy dame."

"I want to go back to see her," said Edward. "I didn't think I should ever see her again. Now she's free and anyone can see her."

He was much pleased that his host thought he was in love with Rhoda. He felt that the thing gave him a halo of interest and pathos. He thought that the saloon keeper would describe the incident to other customers later in the day. "Had a guy in here . . . picks up the *Examiner* . . . intellectual looking guy too . . ."

"I want to go back to her," said Edward, "but I haven't a cent. That is to say, of course, I have ten—enough, I hope, to pay for the brandy."

"The brandy's two bits," amended his host doubtfully. "That's too bad. How come?"

"I bicycled here."

There was a considerable pause.

"You don't want to buy a book called *Milton for Boys?* I'm a salesman. I've struck hard times."

"Why, no," said the saloon keeper, whose manner was now rather colder. "We don't have no use for books, not in my lina business."

Edward clung to the counter. He would never leave it without money, he thought hysterically. The saloon keeper went and served another customer, whistling doubtfully as he did so. Then he produced an account book and began writing down figures. Edward held the counter tightly. He began to feel faint with hunger and excitement. A noise like mowing machines on summer lawns at home was in his ears. The saloon keeper finally looked at him.

"Want something to eat, brother?" he asked. "I'd be willing."

"No," said Edward. He felt vaguely that to accept food would lessen the force of his appeal. There was a hopeless silence again. Edward's head drooped over the counter. He seemed to be looking closely at the grain of the wood.

"The man must be touched by this," he thought

dimly. "I must look awfully white by now." There was a freezing feeling on the skin of his face.

"Now, see here, young feller," said the saloon keeper. "I hate to see you in bad. I've got a soft heart, so the boys tell me. I'd kinda hate to have a foreigner quit this city feeling mean like you feel right now. I kin size up a man that's on the level as well as anyone. Now this is what I'll do. You let me see this wheel of yours and I don't say but what I kin loan you a few bucks on it."

Edward leaned on the counter for a minute more. "I might be able to redeem it," he thought. "Anyway Cliff said I'd probably skip with it, so he won't be surprised. It's a little thing to do—for Emily."

He wheeled the bicycle into the bar.

"Gee, she's had some knocks," said the saloon keeper. He came round the counter and rang the bell of the bicycle. "Next time you come around this ways, mebbe . . . well, brother, I'll trust you. You kin have a hot dog on me and a cup-a coffee. I'll loan you a coupla bucks on it. That'll take you as far as Frisco."

"Obstacles are nothing to Our Hero," thought Edward and then, "Cliff won't be surprised. Nor will Pop. Pop will say 'That's what comes of picking up with a Britisher.' He'll spit and pretend he's spitting on England."

San Francisco seemed to Edward to be set in pearls. Pearl clouds bowled about the hills; the bay and the Golden Gate had the opaque glow of pearls.

The little tram lifted him up the steep streets towards Rhoda—no, towards Emily. From the top of the straight hill he saw the city lying in curious leaning perspectives. Houses on other hills seemed built upon each other like the stones of great pyramids. The air was full of white sun and all the shadows were trim.

Misgivings met him halfway up the wooden outside stairway that led to Rhoda's door.

No-one answered the bell. He could not believe the silence. He rang again and again. No-one answered.

He stood on the stairs with an empty mind. Then he began to remember running down those stairs, pursuing Emily after his first meeting with her. It seemed to him now that he had not loved her at all while she had been here, within reach. He could not remember his past feelings. He could remember nothing but looking at her. The Edward of those days was a blank to him now. He had lived then outside himself, living austerely on the intermittent sight of her. Now he could not even remember what it was that he had seen in her face, he could not remember what it was that gave her eyes that starred look. Was it because they were set so deep under her strong black brows?

The janitress stood at the foot of the stairs. "Mrs. Bird ain't to home. Gawn south somewheres in Louisiana. Didn't you-all see it in the paper? She done had a collapse."

Edward did not answer. He looked down at the janitress. He could not see her feet; he was so steeply above her. He could see, however, that some of her hair was false and did not match the rest. After a minute she was gone.

Avery Bird had come half-way up the wooden stairs before Edward really believed that he was there.

They looked at each other in unfriendly silence.

Avery looked frantic; his face was a yellowish white; his thick lips were fixed in a straight line; his cheeks were as hollow as though he were sucking them in. Even his curly black hair looked crushed.

After he had looked at Edward for a minute he pushed by him and unlocked the door.

"Can't you leave us alone?" he said.

Edward seemed to himself to dwindle. He could hardly believe that anyone had spoken so. "Our Hero—what? Are heroes so addressed? *Can't you leave us alone?* It is intolerable. I am an absolute and appalling failure."

With a limp hand he reached for the door as Avery shut it against him. He touched the door in a yielding way as a cat would touch it. The touch was like magic. Avery opened the door again. "Come in, come in. Oh, come in, come in," he said furiously. As he preceded Edward into the studio he went on saying, "Come in, come in, oh come in. . . ." Poor Edward was coming in as

155

quickly as he could. Dirty cups and plates were all over the studio. The shades were down over all the windows but one.

"I detest the sight of you," said Avery. "You are like a beastly disease in my house. You worried Rhoda till she cried at night. Now she is gone, to cry in another bed."

"I don't know what you mean."

Avery did not know altogether what he meant. There was to him something hideous and detestable about Edward. Edward had been too much in his sight. Avery was full of Jewish vigour himself; the poorness and the pimples, the thinness and the hesitancy of Edward were revolting to him.

"You don't know what I mean? Didn't you know that Rhoda would have *paid* to get you out of this country, out of her sight, out of the sight of all decent people."

Edward did not speak of the suggested commission to take Rhoda's pictures to China. He knew very well that Avery was right. Rhoda would have paid to get him out of her sight. That was all she had meant. Her pictures, bad, mad, careful pictures, were still on the wall.

"Now she has gone," said Avery. "She has forgotten me—she has worse than forgotten you."

"Gone . . . forgotten?" Edward thought. He could not connect violent words with the serene and reasonable Rhoda. He could not imagine her sturdy neat face distorted by fury or hysteria.

Avery said, "What do you want? Are you begging for her money again?"

"Yes," said Edward. He sank down into a mire of disgust. He was feeling sick.

Avery snatched at a wallet on the table. He threw all the papers from it to the floor and there was a roll of money clinging to the brim of the wallet. "Take it, take it, take it, take it!" he shouted, slamming down one fifty dollar bill after another among the reeling cups on the table. "Oh, take it, take it, take it! . . ."

Edward was taking it as quickly as he could.

"And for Christ's sake get off this side of the world," added Avery. "You . . . gopher."

Edward backed a few paces towards the door. Avery laughed. His face was twitching; his eyes were burning red. He looked very ugly and almost childish and Edward, as he realised this, felt braver. He stood with his back to the door. He knew very well that when he had disappeared, Avery would put his head down among the unwashed cups. Why, the man was already crying.

"You have been exceedingly rude to me," said Edward. He thought, "Our Hero threw one contemptuous glance back into the room as he left."

Edward went out. As he closed the door he could hear the cups clash.

CHAPTER SIX

If love be a flower,
Pluck not that flower,
Though flowers be cool
And dear to thy brow.
Thou happy fool,
Thou shalt travel not far,
Thou shalt lie down with this
Cold flower for thy lover.
He shall blind, he shall star
Thine eyes.   His cold kiss
Thy mouth shall cover.

If love be music,
Hear not that music,
Sing not that song,
Though songs be few.
Oh, very strong,
Very close is the weaving
Of notes among notes.
Thou art bound and entangled.
Sing, then, unbelieving,
And sing till thy throat's
Soft song is strangled.

If love be a lion,
Flee not that lion,
Let thy triumphing bones
On the desert lie.
On a desert of stones

THE POOR MAN

Thy bones shall smile,
Comforted only
By stark silence.
Silence and dew
Be thy crown, for thou
Wert blind to a flower
And deaf to music.

EDWARD could hardly believe in his own existence
when he found himself approaching China.

Japan had been nothing. A country packed with
color and little hills but empty of importance, being
empty of Emily. All in vain the veil of Fujiyama
floated over Yokohama; all in vain little pearl-like
clouds were strung round the shoulders of Fujiyama in the indefinite sun. Edward only thought it
was very like its pictures.

When he rode in a little light ricksha through
the centreless streets of Yokohama, he thought,
"This is Edward Williams doing the things that
Sunday school children at home see on lantern slides.
But Our Hero remains detached, as in a dream."
He was glad to feel detached, to feel that, unlike
the other passengers on the ship, he was not "doing
the Orient." He was looking for Emily.

Afterwards he remembered more of Japan than
he had realised at the time. He had been incon-
sistent enough to imitate the majority of the passengers and go by train to Kobe. He had even
been chosen as escort by a stout, lonely lady passenger. "Women were more and more interested in

Our Hero as he grew older and sadder. Women adore an atmosphere of tragedy." It was true that Edward had scarcely been able to hear anything that the lonely lady said. It must therefore have been his "mystic air of remoteness" that had interested her. Or perhaps it was just that he was a man. Together they had spoiled for themselves the enchantment of the Kamikura Buddha by climbing coarsely up the steps inside him. Together, in a hired Ford car, they roared through the faery streets of Kyoto in broad daylight without pausing to hear the clicking pattens in the crowded quiet streets. They did not wait to see the crouching lion outlines of the temples against the multiplying stars of an evening sky. All the flowers of Japan passed Edward by. "I am no botanist," he said proudly.

Japan haunted him afterwards like a ghost. Afterwards he knew that he had shut his eyes. Afterwards he knew that he had nothing to remember, nothing but little sharp negligible details that had pricked his idle mind—the white crests printed on the backs of the blue-clad coolies—the paint on the women's faces—the way the women's toes turned in—the greasiness of the women's hair—the deformed look of the women's backs in the evening when they put on outer kimonos over their broad thick obi sashes—the angry officious voices of the policemen—the similarity of the Tokyo railway to the London Underground. . . .

After rejoining the ship at Kobe he had defiantly

read cheap books all through the Inland Sea. At Nagasaki he did not land. "I'm not a tourist— I'm here on business," he told a little fat bald American business man, who had not asked him whether he were a tourist or not.

Manila Edward ignored. He only saw one thing belonging to Manila, a small Filipino woman with gauze sleeves and ruffles starched as though she were an Elizabethan, who came on board with her husband, a little man, the upper part of whose body was sensibly clothed in a garment of such transparency that no single crease or roll of brown fat over his ribs and stomach was hidden.

And here was Hongkong.

Edward woke up. He was alive to the bland blue outlines of the Peak against the sky. Every scarlet and gold flutter of the paper prayers on the importunate sampans that raced for the liner was a message from Emily to Edward.

People talked with English voices in Hongkong. Edward could hardly hear what the women said. England at last! He followed a couple of pink, small-headed subalterns to the hotel. He heard one say, "By Jove," in a throaty English voice. Edward felt no longer despised and exotic. He saw that everyone in the hotel lobby looked cooler than himself. But the faces were English and not complacent. Or even if they were a little complacent— why not?—they were English. He ordered a cocktail.

"After that I will look in the register," he thought. "Perhaps Emily's name will lie like a strip of light on the first page I look at."

He did not know Emily's last name.

He could hardly believe for a moment that he did not know her name. The cocktail was so good that while he was drinking it he thought, "I shall think of her name in a minute." But nobody had ever told him her name.

"I know Tam's name at least."

It was a pseudonym.

He deliberately interposed a blankness between his brain and this disaster of a China rendered empty of Emily. China to him meant Emily now. The divorce of the two words—China—Emily—was inconceivable.

He studied the register. "If I see her writing I shall recognise it—though I have never seen it."

A long untidy addition sum of names lay before him on the page. The result of the sum was— nothing. He turned to another fruitless page. Another. "Miss E. L. Spring, Walthamstow. . . . Mr. Irwin Scales, Binset, Somerset . . . Mrs. Irwin Scales. . . ." The date of those was about right. E. L. Spring? It was a blasphemy. Walthamstow? . . .

But the date was all right.

E. L. Spring was the only woman with the initial E. There were dark horses all over the page, fiendishly concealing the most important part of their

names . . . Miss Framlingham, Delhi, India . . .
Miss Wherry, London . . . Miss Burnett, Canter-
bury . . . Miss Something Illegible, San Francisco,
Calif. . . . They all sounded like thin women with
withered necks and little green veils hanging from
the backs of their hats, not like Emily.

He returned to the chair beside his empty cocktail glass. His eyes had tears in them so he pretended there was a fly in one of them. His throat
was compressed by distress. He could not have
spoken aloud. "I thought I left myself behind," he
thought. "But I am still Edward Williams in
China. Myself has caught me up. Look at me,
crying now in a hot chair in Hongkong, I who used
to cry in the cold draught that ran through my
dreadful room in San Francisco."

The heat was like stagnant steam. He felt sick
and very deaf. The only sounds he could hear
through the exasperating roaring of his ears were
the sharp cries of the chair-bearers outside the open
window, trying to attract patronage. The cool
vacant faces of English women moved up and down
in the shadow of the arcades outside. Edward could
not hear the clicking of their high heels, they seemed
to him to move subtly like ghosts.

It was terribly hot.

"I shall cry frankly unless I move about." He
hung his self-conscious head as he left the hotel.
He tried to interest himself in the Chinese names
above the shops. No—not China now; China was

a horrible half-name now. The Peak leaned like a cloud over the houses. He could see a little train sliding up the mountain, like a fish which some giant fisherman was drawing up from the sea. He found the station. The train was full, but, as Edward approached it, an official, seeing him, turned out a Chinese clerk in order that Edward might find a place. Edward looked angrily at the patient alert face of the ousted Chinese on the platform. "I don't care if his business is urgent," thought Edward. "I hope his wife is dying. It isn't fair that only I should be hurt."

"Oh, my dear . . ." screamed the hot English girl in front of Edward to her hot friend. All the women in the car were fanning themselves and talking in a frenzy of foolish energy about men.

The car lifted them all up the hill. Dense dull shrubs bordered the steep track. The houses seemed to lean against the hill. The harbour was unrolled at the foot of the mountain. A fringe of ships, like tentacles round a jellyfish, radiated from the shore. Kowloon, backed by crumpled hills, stretched out a corresponding fringe towards Hongkong. Edward's ears cracked and clicked, affected by the change of level.

He walked on the neat paths of the Peak. The Peak seemed as hot as the seashore. "Must be nearer the sun," thought Edward confusedly. But no, it seemed that he was above the sun; he had left the sun behind floating on a thin delicate sea. It was sinking in the sea. All the islands were blue imitative suns, sinking in the sea. The whole sky was the colour of fire. Edward could almost hear the roaring of the fire in the sky. The sea was suddenly sheathed in shadow; mists like snakes writhed between the islands. The islands were no longer sinking in the sea; they were buoyed up by encircling mists. Why was it still so hot? The sea closed and flowed over the sun. The fire in the sky burned no more.

Edward though, "She must have gone to Peking." At once it was cooler. "I will go to Peking tomorrow." At once he began to enjoy the thought of China. A Chinese woman with a small gaunt face in a bright blue tunic and trousers neatly pressed, her sleek black hair in a spangled net, a neat white flower in her hair, tottered by on small compressed feet. He thought "Emily would have wanted to kiss that darling woman. Perhaps she would have kissed her. No, she would have stood and looked back at her, she would have jumped a little and all her body would have been electrified with pleasure. 'Oh, look . . . oh, look . . . oh, look . . .' The woman would have turned and laughed in delight.

He could not believe it when next day a schoolboy English clerk behind a counter told him the price of a journey to Peking.

"Say it again, please," said Edward.

The boy said it again without referring to any

165

book. He seemed to know the dreadful words by heart, just as a torturer knows by heart the levers that will hurt most.

"That's seventy dollars more than I have," said Edward.

"Hard luck," said the boy, looking at him curiously. It seemed odd to him to admit such a thing. "You can go by boat to Tientsin. That would save you a few dollars."

"It wouldn't save enough dollars for me," said Edward. He stood on the doorstep of the office. "Well, I can't stop here all day," he thought. Several times he told himself briskly, "Well, well, well, I can't stop here all day. . . ."

He comforted himself presently by thinking, "I must have tremendous courage to have got so far. Many people wouldn't have got out of that naked little room in San Francisco." He drew a little courage from the illusion of his own courage. Presently he realised that the world did not end on the doorstep of a tourist agency. He found several possible jobs in the newspaper. "English jobs sound somehow less fierce than American jobs," he thought and, buoyed up by a desperate hope, he called on the headmaster of an English school for Chinese.

"I'm afraid you haven't had much experience of teaching," said the headmaster, a gentle, uncertain young man, looking at Edward unhappily.

"It is I who am afraid," replied Edward courteously.

THE POOR MAN

The school was in great need of teachers. The headmaster did not seem to mind whether the teachers could teach—if only a specious appearance of teaching was sustained in his dozen classrooms. Edward was engaged at a small salary to live in the school and teach a class of fifty boys in "all ordinary English subjects." There was one professional teacher in the school—a woman. The other teachers' desks were occupied by one or two unemployed merchant seamen, some bright young women stenographers, a stray woman journalist teaching "as a stunt," and two or three sullen Chinese whose classes were always in an uproar.

Edward nearly fainted as the headmaster took him into the classroom on the first day and introduced him to the boys. "I am sure you will do your best . . . Mr. Williams who lives in England and has spent much time in America . . . giving his time to help Class C in their study of English . . . Now, boys, we must all do our best . . . make Mr. Williams welcome. . . ."

While the headmaster's shy voice wavered on, Edward studied the faces in front of him. Half the class was Eurasian; the other half Chinese. There were one or two thin, glowing Indian faces among the broad Chinese masks. Three Portuguese-Chinese boys in staring striped suits with small waists sat in the front row, trying successfully to frighten Edward by means of an exaggerated look of awe. With these exceptions the two front rows were occupied by little boys who were physically too weak to challenge the determination of the big boys to sit behind unseen. Edward looked hopefully at two little boys in the front row trying to look superlatively good. Their lips were moving; they were making a show of repeating the headmaster's words to themselves in order to make a good impression. Over their heads Edward could see a dazzle of insolent faces, laughing at him and at the futile gentle enthusiasm of the headmaster. The big boys were quite frankly talking. Sometimes even Edward could hear their twanging voices. The headmaster looked wistfully down the room at the disturbers but made no comment. Edward felt his face fixed in an expression that a martyr might wear. His face was frozen. He could not change his expression. He looked in sickly appeal at the headmaster, who was now leaving the room. He looked in sickly appeal at the boys.

There was a fearful silence, broken by one of the big Eurasians at the back suddenly breaking into song.

"Eh—tya—tya . . ."

"Now you must be quiet, please," said Edward huskily.

"Shall not I sing?" enquired the musician. "Am not I having sing lesson every evening when school finish?"

Edward ignored him. "I see by the timetable that we should begin with a Scripture lesson——"

"Oh, no sah—nevah Scriptchah. Monday mornings we was having hygiene—no, we was having dictations—nevah Scriptchah."

The concerted noise of contradiction became louder and louder. Edward felt as if he were caught in a great roaring machine that he could not stop. "Oh, silence . . . oh, silence . . ." he cried, tapping the desk feebly with his pencil. He could not stop the noise. He rose and flung his arms out. "Oh, silence—I can't stand this."

The hysterical gesture produced a startling silence. Then some of the big boys laughed.

"The timetable says Scripture and I say Scripture," said Edward furiously. "No-one else's opinion is needed. Now I want one of you big boys—I don't know your names yet—that one with a pale blue coat on—to come and tell me how far you got in the Bible . . ."

"Please sah, you say no other man opinion was needed."

"Shut up, curse you."

"Eh—tya—tya . . ."

"He sing a song for welcoming you, sah."

The boy in a long pale blue coat stood in front of Edward, unexpectedly abashed. His small eyes seemed deliberately veiled with dulness.

"What is your name?" asked Edward.

"I new scholar."

"You have a name, though," insisted Edward.

"Oh, no, sah," shouted another boy from the back

169

of the room. "He was having no name. He was married man . . ."

"His name was Ng Sik Wong," said one of the laboriously good little boys.

"*What* is his first name?"

"Ng," buzzed the whole class.

"I can't believe it." Feeling a little braver Edward wrote down, ? Sick Wong—Scar on nose—pale blue—halfwitted," in his notebook. "Now, . . . ahem, Sick Wong, you're one of the biggest boys in the class, aren't you?"

"I new scholar."

"Almost big enough to be a master, eh?"

"Eh—tya—tya . . . Hey, Ng Sik Wong—you be master—number one class master—married man . . ."

Edward pressed on. "So I'm sure I can depend on you to try and help me."

"I new scholar."

"Go back to your seat."

"Please, sah," cooed a good little boy. "I shall help you. I shall tell you where was we reading holy book. Last Monday we have finish Matthew-holy-gospel-according-to twenty four chapter. I tell you my name, sah. I Rupert Frazer, sah."

Open your Bibles at the twenty fifth chapter of Saint Matthew."

Bibles flew about in the air. There was a riotous noise of opening books and a few whines, "Please sah, he steal my book . . . please sah, Pong Poon

Chong pinch me . . . Sah, I have lose my Bible since a long time . . ." The tallest of the smart Portuguese boys in the front row rose.

"Excuse me, sah, what does it mean, Virgin?"

Edward's skull was sweating. "A virgin—" he began.

"Eh—tya—tya . . ."

"Surely the whole class has sense enough not to ask silly questions."

"Please, sah, you shall tell him ask Ng Sik Wong. He married man."

"Please, sah, tell him ask Ng Sik Wong wife—she shall know what is virgin—I wonder . . ."

"A virgin is a young unmarried woman," said Edward, petulantly damning all virgins.

"But, sah——"

"In this case that definition is enough."

"But, please, sah——"

"Begin to read, Rupert Frazer."

In a high staccato voice which ignored punctuation and sense, Rupert Frazer began to read.

"Please, sah," said the tallest of the three Portuguese. "Please excuse us leave the room, sah." All three rose as if worked by one lever.

"What for?" asked Edward.

"Eh—tya—tya . . ."

The three Portuguese stared at Edward in exaggerated reproach and bashfulness.

("And att midnight there wass a cry made behold de brid-a-groom cometh go yee—")

"Very well. Come straight back," said Edward.

("Less thah bee no eno for uss and—")

"Oh, stop, Frazer," implored Edward. "Next boy, read."

The boys on Frazer's right and left began reading in concert with furious glances at each other.

"Not both; the Indian boy."

"I am Parsee," said the boy, a small nervous looking child. "My name iss Bannerjee."

"Please excuse us leave the room, sah," said the first of a line of big boys filing past Edward's desk towards the door.

"Stop," shouted Edward unsteadily. His head was rocking with the heat and consciousness of failure. "Go back to your seats."

"Oh, sah, other teachah Mistah Ramsee he nevah stop us."

"Go on reading, Bannerjee," said Edward. He pretended not to see the last of the line disappearing through the door. The departure of the disturbing element gave rise to peace in the class.

"Watch therefore," read a boy with a Chinese face and a German accent. "For ye know neither the day nor the hour wherein the Son of Man cometh. Please, sah, is not it true dat nuns haf Our Lord als Bridegroom?"

"Nuns iss virgins," said one of the Parsees in a shocked voice.

"Please, sah," continued the German. "Iss it not

Mystic Union between Our Lord and nuns? If we not believing in Mystic Union between Holy Lord and mankind iss it not true we shall be perishing in outer darkness and there shall be whipping and gnashing off teeth?"

"Everyone is free to have his own opinion about these things," said Edward, doubtfully. "Outer darkness is only a parable in itself——"

"But the Bible say——"

"There are a great many interpretations of the Bible's words," snapped Edward, feeling unhappy and strangely alone among the quiet familiar words in front of him. "Perhaps we should all be more likely to agree on the general sense of this parable. What do you think Jesus meant us to understand by this story——"

"Not story, sah, it was holy parable."

"Well, what can we learn from this parable?"

"We shall not know, sah. You telling us, after—we shall be knowing."

"Use your minds. What lesson do you find in the parable?"

"We not virgins, sah."

"Mistah Ramsee he nevah ask the thing he have not teach."

"This is Mr. Williams, not Mr. Ramsay," said Edward, whose confidence was increasing with the increasing tranquillity of the class. "I will give you three minutes in which to glance over the parable again before answering——"

"It mean—the wicked people shall perishing in efferlasting fires," declaimed the German.

"Silence for three minutes."

There was an uneasy silence broken suddenly by the opening of a side door. The woman teacher in the next classroom stood in the doorway and spoke in a contemptuous voice to Edward. "Will you please restrain your boys from shooting their pea-shooters at this door? The noise in the next room is most disturbing."

"Sorry," said Edward, feeling lost again. "I'm rather deaf. I didn't know . . ."

"And you might like to know," continued the visitor, "that eleven boys from this class are playing ball in the playground. I don't know, of course, if they have your permission . . ."

"Oh, well . . ." said Edward. "My God, it's ter-ribly hot, isn't it? . . ."

The woman-teacher shut the door sharply.

Edward felt as if he were outside himself, as if he could see himself leaning limply over his desk, his damp mud-colored hair drooping forward—its parting lost—his thin face shining with sweat and almost certainly rather dirty, the red spots growing redder upon his chin and forehead, his lower jaw trembling although he was trying, by hard biting, to hold it steady. "Even if I found Emily," he thought, "she would hate me now." He could never be cool or lovable in these thick weary English clothes. Then he thought with sudden pleasure that he would buy a new suit, a cool pale suit in which to meet Emily. He imagined himself, looking delicate and tired and cool in a delicately pale suit, walking triumphantly towards Emily along a Chinese street between booths full of lilies. "Oh, look . . . oh, look . . ." Emily would cry, throwing her arms up in her exquisitely exaggerated way. "Oh, look . . . here's that darling Edward . . . looking like a damned old primrose . . ."

"Shall I went to tell Ma Lo Yung and other boys come in to lesson?" suggested the saintly Rupert Frazer.

"Yes, run along for Heaven's sake," said Edward, trembling with various emotions.

The day was at last over. It seemed like two days to Edward because it was cut in half by an hour for luncheon. During this hour he could be sullen and quiet; the half dozen other men teachers took little notice of him. The women teachers could be heard screaming in secluded mirth in another room.

The week was at last over. Edward had half Saturday and all Sunday to himself. Not quite to himself, for on Sunday he had to be "on duty" for half the day. He sat in the window of his room in the shade of the big palm-tree outside. Heat hummed through the garden, through the open doors and along the dingy passages of the school. Edward did not mind what the boys were doing—whatever it was, they were doing it fairly quietly.

Occasionally a tearing yell of laughter or a whine or a shrill protest in Chinese was mixed with the hum of heat and insects.

Edward was comforted by comforting spirits, the contents of two bottles which were his only contribution to the furniture of his room. These represented the only money he had spent that week. The new suit was still a dream. He taught in his shirt-sleeves.

He had nothing to do on Sundays. Yet he tried to regulate his drinking. He made appointments with himself. "At half past three I will have another . . ." But sometimes he forgot and had another too early. "It keeps off the mosquitoes," he thought.

One of the big Portuguese boys from his class was standing in the doorway. "Please, Mistah Weelims . . ."

"Have a drink," said Edward. He thought the boy looked rather beautiful; his black hair was so thick and shining; it was brushed like a smooth breaking wave.

Before suppertime there were six boys in Edward's room. "If you fellers would only behave decently in class," said Edward, feeling like a man of the world surrounded by his friends, "we'd have s'more parties like this . . ."

Edward stayed at the school for a month. The boys were almost fatherly to him. Edward ceased to assert authority. His system was based entirely on bribes. The system seemed to answer. Only once during the month the headmaster sent a note to ask that less noise be made in Class C. That was when a boy hid behind the blackboard and overturned it upon Edward. This amused even the good boys.

"A joke's a joke," said Edward with tears in his eyes. The blackboard had shaken tears into his eyes. Two of the big boys had their arms around his neck, were roaring yells of laughter into his ear. "This joke's certainly on me. Oh, come now, go easy." He was straining after laughter. He thought, "That's the way to take boys, no frills, no airs . . ." He thought he was fond of the boys. He knew they were not fond of him. He was terribly afraid of them. The note from the headmaster was handed to him.

"A letter from Daisy . . . he says we're making too much noise, fellers."

He did not drink much in the day-time. Whisky in such hot weather made him tremble, made him unable to bear the noise and difficulty of the class room. But after dinner, when at least it was dark and one could pretend that the heat was lifted, he drank a good deal and was comforted. But he saved a great deal of his salary. He thought he would look for an opportunity to leave. He would be ill; it was quite easy for him to seem ill. He would be obliged to go and see a great American doctor in Peking about his hearing. He had been

engaged for three months, in the absence on sick
leave of one of the regular teachers, but he had no
sense of responsibility to the school. His brain was
full of prospective interviews with the headmaster.
"I suffer terribly with my ears and my sinuses. I
have just had a most dangerous operation. I need
hardly say it will be a matter of real regret to me
to leave the dear boys. . . ." The headmaster
would say, "Of course, of course, I quite understand." Edward had not only no objection to telling lies, he even failed as a rule to notice how
broadly he lied.

He did not have a chance to excite the sympathy
of the headmaster. He was turned out of the school
one Sunday.

Sunday was his day without fear, and when he
was on duty on Sunday afternoons, he drank a great
deal. His last Sunday passed like a dream; he had
no fear except the fear of the week to come. He
was aware that he was to preside at the supper of
the boarders. The half-dozen big boys who had
been "sharing the party" thought he had forgotten.
Edward laughed at this idea. The big boys shep-
herded him downstairs to the dining room; they
linked their arms with his in facetious tenderness.
It was absurd, Edward thought. His mind was
quite clear and serene. He knew that he would have
to say grace. The boys' food was very bad—the
boys told him so. How absurd to say grace over a
bad meal. Indeed it was blasphemy. He would be

honest. He would be witty. What a curious perspective of white faces along the tables. The boys
spoiled the austerity of the perspective by wearing
different-colored clothes.

"Let us pray that dinner today will be better than
it was yesterday." (God does not mind a man being
witty at His expense.) "O God, who daily turnest
our bread into a stone———"

Well, even if the Matron was looking at him, she
could appreciate wit, couldn't she? He laughed a
little to give her a lead. Her hard white collar and
cap seemed to heave like the ruff and crest of an
affronted bird. Women had no sense of humor.
And anyway it was *he*, not *she*, who was on duty.
He could say what grace he liked. The matron was
gone now. She had realised that she had no business there. The boys were all laughing. They were
a broad-minded crew, these boys.

Someone took him quite rudely by the arm. It
was the headmaster. He looked drunk, Edward
thought. So that was how the headmaster spent
Sunday afternoons—and he a parson. He pulled
Edward out of the room. It was outrageous that
the headmaster should so interrupt Edward's
duties.

After a short talk, during which the headmaster
gave voice to some most insolent personalities, Edward realised quite suddenly that he himself was
drunk. He wanted immediately to go away from
the people who had noticed this humiliating fact.

He wanted new faces around him, unreproachful faces.

"I'm going," said Edward; the chair span away from him unkindly as he rose. "After the way I've been treated——"

"Please go tonight," said the headmaster.

Everything was going well. Soon he would be away from these people who only witnessed his moments of indignity. The boys would never triumph over him again now. He would be alone, travelling in search of Emily. People who did not know him would think, "Who is that thin eager young man with the far-off look in his eyes?"

The Matron packed his clothes for him. She did not speak. She touched his possessions as though they were dirty. The headmaster called a ricksha for him and, without speaking, put Edward's suitcase into it. Nobody said good-bye. The stars were like dew on Edward's eyes. Inside his head pulsed the impact of the ricksha coolie's feet on the ground. The street was narrow and crowded and quiet, at least there were only voices in it. Across the lighted booths and under the hanging bannered shop signs hurried the coolies at a half trot on their bare feet. Their burdens swung at either end of long poles; they had slung the great absurd shields which were their hats on their backs, the heat of the day being over. "Hai-ya ho, hoi-ya hai-ya, hai-ya ho, hoi-ya hai-ya. . . ." Two withered women, with thin bare legs under their turned-up trousers, were beating a child's garment with poles. Fierce treatment for so small a thing. But the devil of sickness was in the garment; it required fierce treatment. The lights glared on the scarlet and gold banners and on the gilt filigree woodwork that framed the doors of the shops. It seemed as if one heard noise more with one's eyes than with one's ears. The glare seemed to drown the voices and the barefoot tread of the crowds. Wherever one street crossed another, however, there was a great clamoring of coolies forging their own right of way through the tangle. Edward's ricksha coolie said "Hao hao" when anyone crossed his path; the "hao" was always in time with the thumping of his running feet, as if jerked from his throat. Tall Sikh policemen pushed coolies roughly about. In the sight of the policemen the little crowd of almost naked beggar children running after Edward momentarily evaporated.

Edward could now pay for his passage to Tientsin by sea and for a ticket from Tientsin to Peking. He could not pay for the new cool suit of clothes. Emily must take him as he was—hot or cold.

He was the only passenger in the ship to Tientsin. It was carrying simply a great deal of indigo—and Edward. It was intent upon this duty and stopped at only one port.

A gentle and pleasant measure of eternity passed over Edward. He lay on a chair alone upon the deck, flattened between the soft sea and sky. Fly-

ing fish rained upwards out of the sea. The flying
fish made little scratches on the smooth sea. One
evening the ship passed the mouth of the Yangtze
River at sunset. An enormous plume of crimson
cloud leaned away from the sea up the river. Thick
polished plates of gold and crimson seemed laid
upon the smooth waves of the sea to the west. The
low hills at the mouth of the river were luminously
purple. . . .

For many days the ship followed the coast, followed it far off, like the timid disciple. There were
high unreasonable islands, suddenly before the un-
suspecting ship. The islands sustained an illusion
of life on their shores; they sent their hopes out
into the sea in little fishing boats. Once there was
a boat quite near. In it one man smoothed his long
unbound hair into a queue; another played on a
stringed instrument and whined a song; another indolently directed the boat towards the bristling
stockade of floating poles that marked their net.
But it must all have been faery. No community
could really live such a secret life, a life so full of
things that would never be known.

One day passengers came on board in mid-sea, a
great crowd of birds, land-birds who knew nothing
of the dangerous skies over the sea. Hawks and
woodpeckers, sparrows and doves and little tits and
finches stood about the rigging pretending not to see
one another. The seagulls laughed at them. The
land-birds felt uneasy standing in these strange,

black, even trees, they were too much puzzled to be very much afraid of men. A red and green bird walked about near Edward, hoping that it would find a worm somewhere. Whenever Edward spoke to it, it pulled itself self-consciuosly together but did not fly away. A Chinese sailor caught a sparrowhawk and tied it to the capstan by the leg. Wei-hai-wei seemed to be the arranged destination of these passengers. Like a Cook's Conducted Tour they all disembarked together in the most business-like way. Only the hawk, tied by the leg to the capstan, was left behind looking sullenly across at the sullen dark battleships that peered out of the harbour.

The three officers of the ship left Edward a great deal alone. The captain was an Irishman, a fat, fair man with great, serene, grey eyes. He had once been, he told Edward pointedly, a slave to drink; he had an idea that Edward was similarly bound. He thought he could haul Edward's soul to safety on a thin string of sentimental reminders . . . "mother, waiting at home . . . grey hairs in sorrow to the grave . . . England needs strong sane men now . . . devil's brew . . . I know, me lad, I've been through hell on account of it. . . ."

"Hell's the word," said Edward placidly, basking in the light of the captain's earnest missionary interest.

The captain would not allow Edward to drink, either in the ship or at Chefoo—their only port of

call. "You don't know China," said the captain.
"You youngsters simply don't know how to behave
in China. In London now, two or three whiskies
and sodas . . . no harm at all. But in China—I
tell you I've seen men arrive in Shanghai with babies'
complexions . . . and five years after . . . yellow
as a daffodil, bent, malarial, only fit for nursing
homes."

Edward hoped that he would look only fit for a
nursing home when he met Emily. Then she would
think, "How he has suffered. How I have made
him suffer."

Much of the indigo disembarked at Chefoo. The
ship seemed to have run aground on a brown island
of barges. This island was peopled by brown coolies with vacant faces; their heads were half shaven
and half covered with hair like cotton waste; sometimes they had bound their hair into chignons.
Under their unresting but unhurrying hands, their
island of barges became mountainous with sacks of
indigo. Many of the sacks burst; indigo oozed
down the slopes of the mountains; the coolies became bluer and bluer; there was indigo in their hair
and indigo round their shoulders like shawls.

Edward and the captain walked austerely and
thirstily about Chefoo. The Chinese of Chefoo
seemed to be of a rougher race than those of Hongkong. They even grated on the eye, Edward
thought. They were taller and hairier; their
clothes were neither neat nor complete. Their

houses were ragged and indecent. The houses of
the missionaries looked to Edward even more impossible than those of the Chinese. Outside one of
the mission gates a thin boy, quite naked, tortured
a yellow lizard. There were yellow, scarred hills
round the harbour. They trailed a silken hem of
white sand into the sea and, behind the town, a green
scarf of orchard land was thrown upon the shoulder
of a low hill.

Between golden castled hills the ship left the harbour in the evening.

The Yellow Sea was really yellow. It was thickly
yellow and reflected no light. It was more like a
desert than a sea. The eye would have found a
string of camels crossing the sea no anomaly.

The Pei-ho River was yellow too. The ship entered the river between low mud forts. Salt was
stacked on a broad streaky plain to the north. Primitive windmills, like merry-go-rounds at English
fairs, whirled among the stacks of salt. The earth
was yellow, the water was yellow, the long slanted
wave that ran after the ship was yellow and, breaking over the squeaking yellow babies on the shore,
left them a little yellower. The villages were of
yellow mud; the blind mud houses had no angles;
they were like beehives. There was a ragged yellow camel kneeling self-consciously in a street; he
kneeled as though his hind legs were broken. A
little girl in dark strawberry red—an exquisite color
for a dweller in golden mud—watched the camel

from a dark doorway. The boats in the river had nets stretched between bending slim poles hinged to their masts. When, worked by primitive levers, these nets were bowed to the water and rose spangled and silvered, the boats were like dragon-flies resting delicately on the water.

Tientsin . . . a few dusty hours in a train . . . Peking. The train seemed to collide with Peking. The high city wall approached the railroad at a steep angle. The train seemed to glance from the wall without impact. Edward found himself outside the Water Gate, at the inner wall of Peking.

He became a ghost in a soundless ricksha. Lights pricked his eyes. There was nothing in this Peking but houses transplanted from European suburbs. There was an English bank, there were English business men, English soldiers, French soldiers, small serene policemen in commonplace khaki uniform, several Chevrolet cars . . . finally an immense hotel, the road to which was lined by rickshas at rest with sweating coolies sitting on their shafts.

"Emily can't be here. This is not Peking. Peking has been stolen away. Emily has been stolen away."

Edward took a room in the hotel. He did not know how he would pay for it. He thought he would be here forever; he hoped that he would soon die; perhaps, through dimming eyes, he would see at last the real Peking and Emily running urgently towards him. "Too late, Emily . . . too late. . . ."

The great lobby of the hotel was like purgatory. Surely it would have held all the saints and sinners of the world. The saints and sinners sat in large absorbing chairs and at little tables, waiting till the time came when they might do something else. There was dance music in the distance, a beat like a hammer behind one's head. The beat fought with the beat of Edward's heart; it was intolerable. He could hear and feel the beat of his heart louder and louder as he drank cocktail after cocktail. Cocktails here at any rate were better than they would have been had he found the real Peking. A broad serene face crowning a high-necked robe of green gold filled Edward's imagination when he thought of Peking. Over that face a banner waved, and as it waved the wild gold dragon on the banner whipped his length about but could not escape. Even the man who brought another cocktail had something to say about this dragon, Edward thought. "The moon is his saddle . . ." the cocktail man seemed to say. It was true; the dragon was saddled by the curve of the satiny moon. Edward had seen the moon from the other side of the Water Gate, when the real Peking had still seemed to be in front of him. Perhaps he could find Peking after all, in the light of the young moon. It was very late. There was hardly time to go to bed, not time, in his present mood, to take off one damp, snarling garment after another, to wash his hot and tired body, to find his way uncertainly into an unknown bed. It would be morning in a breath.

He went out. He walked east. The air was cool and the sharp brittle rays of the stars made him feel as though he were on the verge of being more widely awake than ever man was before. Here were trees and a very broad moonlit street. Here, suddenly, was Peking. A great gate cast its mountainous tented shadow to his feet. The curves of the roofs above the gate were high and ample and optimistic. The moon shone through the deserted windows of the high guard-house. There were soldiers at the gate so Edward went no nearer to its arch. But he waded in its clean shadow upon the uneven dust of the street. He walked still east, along very narrow streets. There were no straight roofs at all; all the eaves turned up as if the roofs were of drooping dark silk with their hems slung to the stars, or as if the houses were dancing and swinging gay skirts.

There was an open space; low trees splashed shadows on white dust and wet grass. Peking was not so tightly packed within its walls but that a wide space might be left in the angle of one corner of the walls, a space where goats and donkeys had their lodging. Beggars slept here too, but Edward's tread on the dust did not wake them.

The walls barred his way. They were new-looking walls, he thought, almost silver in the moon-

light, the design of castellation fencing the outer rim
was unbroken. But the guard-house on the corner
of the wall looked forgotten and old. There was
a brick slope which climbed to the top of the wall.
Iron gates barred both the foot and the head of the
slope, but the gates were easily climbed.

Edward was on the broad weedy path that ran on
the top of the wall. The seeds of flowers and tall
grasses had accepted the wall as part of the soil of
China. Edward went into the high beamed hall of
the guard-house. The moonlight made strange and
glorious broad spaces of its dusty floor; its dazzled
windows looked out on naked moonlight. It was
so full of silence that its old walls cracked.

That corner of Peking was a watching corner. A
little further on the dragons of the Observatory
watched the stars. Great wild bucking dragons
bore on their backs or between their claws huge
secret instruments which, in the belief of men and
dragons, prepare the way of the Lord and make his
paths straight. The bronze dragons of the Peking
Observatory are only a little junior to history, but
Edward did not know that. He tried feebly to open
the locked gate and then forgot and left the dragons, the spying and puritan dragons, holding their
check on the wild and dancing stars.

To the west Peking was like an enchanted forest
in the milky half light. No house declared itself
among the trees except the great insolent hotel which
raised itself like a banner of unworthy victory over

the quiet city. Beyond Peking, far away, were the Western Hills, their outline a wild tossing together of angles, their chequered surface broken by strange folds and scars.

There was a light other than the moon. It was not a sudden light but Edward realised it suddenly. The dawn was creeping up behind him to devour him unawares. The centre of the universe had shifted. The dawn was a subtler miracle than was the moon; the dawn succeeded to the empire of the moon.

Light ran like a snake along the tops of the Western Hills. There was a spear of flame along the eastern horizon. Little escaping clouds caught fire; there was an ominous look of molten gold where the east made ready the first step of the stair for the sun's ascent. The sun pointed its sword abruptly at Peking. The golden roofs of the Imperial City most gloriously received the challenge. The city threw away its cloak of mystery and the birds sang. A blue cart, its long peak stretching forward as far as the ears of the mule that drew it, its little fretted windows set into the blue tunnel that covered it, heaved slowly along a red track from the east into the sunstricken city.

The dam of day had burst.

Edward thought, "Emily is somewhere, drowning, asleep in that lake of sunlight. I can find her now. I have begun finding instead of losing now. . . ."

Where does hope set its roots? Out of what

blessed and silly seed does hope rise like a flower,
fed by nothing more reasonable than a piercing of
sunlight through air full of birds' songs? It is
curious how joyfully we pluck and wear at our hearts
that fatal hope that has sprung from the seed of a
dream or of the little wind that passes across the
morning.

"Hope is a true thing," thought Edward when he
looked, later in the morning, at the hotel register.
There were the names.

> "Mr. and Mrs. Tam McTab—not so well but
> unfortunately more correctly known as
> Mr. and Mrs. Leslie Watson—" (Tam had
> written facetiously).
> "Miss Emily Frere"—(in a small impudent
> writing).
> "Master Stone W. Ponting."

The clerk said that they had left some weeks
ago—here was the date—all except the young gentleman, Master Ponting, he was over there—the one
drinking a lemon squash.

Stone W. Ponting was about thirteen years old;
his thick, upstanding hair seemed gray with dust;
dirt and freckles obscured his complexion; his hands
were dark with dirt.

"You're Stone Ponting, aren't you?" said Edward
nervously. "Mrs. Melsie Ponting's boy?"

"Yump," said Stone, speaking into a glass of
lemon squash.

Edward was afraid of him. He never really believed that boys of thirteen had no longer the power to twist his arms.

"Have you heard your mother speak of me— Edward R. Williams?"

But Stone, who had an abnormally long tongue, was using it to explore the outside of his lower cheek, in the hope of prolonging by a second or two the taste of lemon squash. Apparently failing in this he peeled the paper from a strip of chewing gum and inserted the contents. He did not answer Edward but, on the other hand, did not destroy hope of an answer by shutting his mouth. The chewing gum, though active, remained in the public gaze.

Edward felt helpless but, in such a cause, dared not cease his efforts.

"What's happened to Emily and her friends?" he asked. "Didn't you come here with them?"

"Yump," said Stone. "Hey, boy, gimme my check. I must hustle. Going out horseback riding with the Doc."

A shower of money fell from his pockets as he rose and the re-assembling of this gave Edward an opportunity to speak again.

"No, but truly, I want awfully to know about Emily and the others. I say, if you'll stay and give the Doc a miss for today, we'll go somewhere and find a real American soda fountain."

He thought Stone might strike him. Or perhaps

Stone would simply walk away, dwindle through the door and be lost in the sunlight forever.

"Sure I'll stop," said Stone W. Ponting, putting out his tongue meditatively and sitting down again. "We kin get a dandy nut sundae right here. Nut sundae's mine."

"Why Emerly's went up the Yangtze Ki-yang," he told Edward in reply to three or four more questions. "So's Tam and Lucy. Peking fer mine, I said, when they wanted to have me go withum. My dad's sent me plenty of dough, so I should worry. My dad'll be tickled to death to have me withum. He and Mom bin fighting for the custody of me. Dad won. But he had to go to *Jap*an or some place on business. He's a finan*cier*."

Edward was neither acute enough nor sufficiently interested to notice the sad bleak defences the child had put up for himself against a hard world. Edward thought, "A detestable child. He has too little imagination and too much horse-sense to help me."

"Wasn't Emily supposed to be looking after you?"

Stone gave a sharp cracked laugh. "I guess Mom thought so. Mom's kinda soft. Emerly knows I'm a feller kin look out for himself. Dad wouldn't give a whoop. He don't know yet, but he should worry. He's a financier. He sent me a thousand bucks to blow—till he could come back from Japan. I got the letter, that is to say, it was addressed to Emerly.

193

There was a thousand bucks for her to blow on me insidum. Emerly's a sport, I'll say. She acted like she was leaving me in charge of a dame here—so's Mom wouldn't get mad at her for piking. But there was nothing to that. The other dame don't worry me any."

"She is shameless," thought Edward. "Loving Emily is like loving a tigress." He felt a better man because he loved the shameless Emily. It was like a romance among supermen, he thought.

"Your mother asked *me* once to take care of you and bring you to your father. I had business at the time that prevented me. But she was very anxious that I should. Perhaps she told you——"

"Mebbe," said Stone indifferently. The nut sundae nearly oozed out of his mouth, but was checked by sleight of suction. "She's kinda soft, is Mom."

"You oughtn't to be here by yourself."

"I'm sicka being handed around," said Stone. "Hey, boy, another nut sundae. And then some. I'm a shark for nut sundaes."

"Well, we can be friends anyway," said Edward shyly. "A man can be friends with another man."

Stone took no notice of this. He lifted up the corner of his jacket and licked from it a lump of nut sundae which had accidentally fallen there. Then he walked away, whining a little song.

Edward had not slept at all. The hope he had nursed a few hours earlier seemed divorced from reality. He remembered suddenly something that his mental cowardice had swept from his mind. "Emily loves Tam," he thought, trying to hurt himself as much as possible. "Emily has never thought of me again. She loves Tam. She wants to steal Tam from Lucy. She is shameless. She is full of fury because she has not got Tam. I am to her the least of the people she met over there somewhere in America, while she was engaged in pursuing Tam." He was determined to throw himself into an agony, he was revelling in fatigue and despair. He imagined his next meeting with Emily. Her fierce eyes would detach themselves reluctantly from Tam's face. They would turn cold as they rested on Edward's own face. Edward's face would look dull and pale; he felt very conscious of the lifelessness of his face. He saw himself so grey as to be almost invisible. Near him now there was an arrangement of mirrors that showed him his own rarely seen profile. It was detestable that life— even the mean allowance of life that was his—should be given to so poor a body. His upper lip was too long, it sloped forward without the curve that enlivens most human lips; his chin was thin and fleshless as though made of paper. His face seemed to him hardly a human face. His shoulders were very round. Out of the corner of his eye he watched his reflection in profile present a cocktail glass to that slack sad mouth. Cocktails at least were left to him. Everything that requires only weakness was left to him. "If all this were not so, this is what I would

do." The intensity of his despair was, with the
help of the cocktail, defeating its own ends. . . .
"if love perhaps gave me life . . . if I were as
shameless as she is . . . and if shamelessness could
give me a little of the splendour that it has given
her, this is what I would do . . . I would get control of that thousand dollars . . . I would travel
night and day, in fury and certainty . . . I would
find her on the banks of the river, the high reeds
as high as her head . . . I would walk to her
with a new tread, a heavy, sure, new tread, and
when she looked she might love me or hate me
. . . but she would remember me then." And
now, though he tried again superficially to revive
his luxury of despair, he could not really think
himself despicable. His coward mind leapt at the
accuser from behind, and in the dark and the dust
the accuser was strangled. Edward smiled at the
boy who brought him a fresh cockatil. When he
smiled he saw now that his upper lip curved after
all.

CHAPTER SEVEN

When your songs for me shall be songs that are finished,
When voices shall have left me beyond my retrieving,
When the key shall be turned and my broad world dimin-
  ished,
A dream of the cricket's song shall save me from grieving.

The long locks of the willow-tree are sloped at one angle,
Are swung to one wind, and that wind can awaken
The crickets to their chanting and the fireflies to spangle
The long locks of the willow-trees, shimmering and shaken.

There are dragons in the sky, and the horned moon is a rider,
The horned moon goes riding through gates that break
  asunder.
Stand wide, O ye gates, for the challenger, stand wider,
He goes challenging the dragons, the dragons and the
  thunder.

I am holding, I am hoarding these songs by the million,
For singers grow very wise but hearers grow wiser,
And a thin flute in the dimness of a dragon-decked pavilion
Plays only for my treasuring, for the treasuring of a miser.

When the key shall have turned on me, the silence disarmed
  me,
And gates at my challenging swing no more asunder,
Not mortally—not mortally my enemy shall have harmed
  me,
For I have heard the crickets' songs and the thin flutes and
  the thunder.

THE POOR MAN

In the evening Edward met Stone Ponting in the corridor. The boy looked pale and hysterical.

"I bin out with Doc. He's bin setting me up cocktails. Some drink I'll say. I've had cocktails before, though—a boy and me knoo a man in Sacramento . . . the other feller had a Buick. . . I ain't no sneezing innocent, believe me. . . ."

Edward followed him into his room.

"I'll say I'd be kinda lonesome here, without Doc —him and me's buddies. Emerly was a sport, I'll tell the world. Her and me raised hell in this one-horse city. My, we made ona these Chink traffic cops mad one day, having ricksha races. . . . Doc's a piker. I didn't feel but a little queer after that cocktail and now he says he'll never buy me another. I tell you I ain't no snivelling kid—he's a piker—I feel queer now and no mistake."

He was very sick. Then he began to cry. Edward sat on the edge of the bed and patted the prostrate boy's knee awkwardly. All the time Edward was thinking, "This boy's going to depend on me absolutely within a few hours. A thousand dollars . . . Besides, it's my duty to look after him. Melsie's a friend of mine. . ."

"There must have been poison in that hooch," sobbed Stone. "Mebbe Doc's a thug, after my thousand bucks. . . . 'Sociating with foreigners has ruined him. Emerly was a sport though she was a foreigner . . . My, I'm lonesome without Emerly, I don't mind telling you. Emerly and me was affinities, like Mom and Lon Merriman. But she quit. Doc says women are all that way." He cried again hideously. "She useter kid me along. She useter make up tales about the stunts Tam could put over. She said he was a saint like in the Bible. Her and me was sharks for the polo-game. We useter went and look at the polo-game and she useter kid me along about the things Tam done when he went to the polo-game. It was like the tales in the kid's supplement of the Sunday papers. Once she said he waved his stick and there was eight balls on the field so's all the guys went off quite happy with a ball and they all shot a goal, and often, she said, he'd stick the ball on to the ground by magic and the fellers'd whack at it and whack at it and ride over it and curse at each other for missing it . . . just kid's tales, but the way she telledum just tickled me to death someway. Gee, makes me laugh right now. . . . I don't mind telling you, this is a bum city without Emerly."

He was still crying a little but the effect of the cocktails was wearing off and soon he would hide himself again behind his rude walls.

"Emerly and me was going to take a look-see at the Big Wall. I dunno why she quit. I can go by myself, I guess. I got a thousand bucks. Still, Emerly's a piker."

"You and I'll go and see the Big Wall," said Edward. "You and I'll be buddies now. We'll go tomorrow."

They went to see the Great Wall. Stone Ponting found great pleasure in taking the tickets. Doc came with them, a stout, red, young man with a fixed smile, which only faded during his frequent and earnest seizures of laughter.

They went up to the pass on a pig train from Nankow; they sat on the running board of the train and their sight was haunted by walls creeping furtively round the mountains and by dead walled towns.

The Great Wall, however, was not furtive. It gloried in its fight with the mountains. It condescended to conquer only the fiercest slopes. It pursued splendidly terrible edges. Edward, looking down from the broad road on the wall at the pale bleak valleys towards Manchuria, was oppressed by a sense of tottering and fearful height. But when he leaned over the battlements and looked down expecting to see straight into dark, dragon-haunted abysses, there was the grass like an assurance of safety a few feet below him, and there were the little intimate blue and yellow flowers in the grass, holding out hands to break the fall of courage. All the way down the steep mountains there were flowers among the rocks. The rocks might have been the graves of enemies of China who had failed and fallen on the green grass, failed and fallen and never set foot on the land within the wall. The wall itself was low; it lay flat like a snake in the sun; it was more sinuous than anything built of brick had any right to be. When it linked crag with crag it was so steep that, to follow it, travellers must sometimes crawl on hands and knees up very steep steps, clinging to the rank weeds and grasses that grew between steep stones. Astride of the wall, at regular intervals, were the watch-towers, entered by arched doorways. The wall looped its length sometimes; there were wanderings of walls within the wall. Wherever one looked the mountains were crowned and mocked by the wall.

Doc hardly had time to look at the wall, he was so busy photographing it.

Stone was frankly bored.

"Can't be but a dozen feet high," he complained. "They ought to see the Capitol at Sacramento or some of the buildings on Montgomery Street in Frisco."

They walked down to the train along the paved camel road that for two thousand years has carried travellers from Manchuria to Peking. It is a dead road now. Occasionally a string of camels or donkeys threads its way through the crowds of travelling ghosts, but a Ford car would disdain the road now, so it is dead.

Doc's Chinese boy, an efficient, cheerful old man who never apparently opened his eyes, was waiting for the three travellers at Nankow with a string of donkeys. Stone proudly produced money whenever it was needed, and Edward had nothing to do except humour Doc's passion for photography. Edward was certain, even while posing with a self-conscious smile between two donkeys, that, by the time the films were developed, Doc would have forgotten the very name of Edward R. Williams. The snapshot, stuck in an album, would be introduced to friends as "Yes, that's a feller—I forgot his name —anyway we were starting off on donkeys—I forget where to. . ." The snapshottist is the most catholic of all artists.

They rode first through Kao-liang and then through orchards to the Ming tombs. Each rider rode in a little dream of donkey bells and of affectionate conversation between the donkeys and the running drivers. The drivers said "Trrk trrk" and "K'erh-to" and "Tsou-pa" and "Yueh," and the donkeys danced along, crossing their delicate little hoofs as if on a tight rope, and signalling with their soft dusty ears.

> Very close to a road of rust,
> Very close to the red ground,
> Till he dies he dwells
> In the dust
> Of his donkey's feet, in the sound
> Of his donkey's bells. . . .

The travellers reached the Ming tombs at sunset. The precarious last light of the sun was spilled over the shining golden roofs. There was a master tomb crouching among its many courtyards, and the disciple tombs on the wooded slopes imitated it respectfully. The marble steps and the carved and knotted marble balustrades seemed to hold light. In the main hall of the main tomb great plain trunks of trees were the pillars bridging the dusky air between the candle-lit pavement and the ceiling. A little marble empty coffin in the innermost place was the only reminder of the fact that the brittle and ridiculous bones of a dead man were the treasure in this sombre splendid casket. This was man's defence against his smallness. "Never dust to dust now," said the dust of the dead Emperor. But his defence was crumbling. The marble and gold pavilion and the years were playing him false.

Edward could not sleep on his camp bed between the great pillars of the entrance. He leaned his chin upon the marble balustrade and watched the darkness. The writhing outlines of cedars and pavilions in the starlight were gold no more. The dragons and the branches of the cedars wrestled together in the dark and were entangled.

Edward was desperately patient with Stone Ponting. He was comforted in this period of doubt by the constant mention of Emily, but he knew Stone well enough now never to suggest that they should go together in search of her. It was impossible for Edward to be charming and Stone did not care for him at all. But they both tried to disguise foolishly delighted smiles when Emily's name was mentioned, and both were conscious of the impossibility of boring each other on a topic which both took pains to introduce.

THE POOR MAN

They rode together in Peking. Edward was a bad horseman but he always felt rather heroic on a horse. They rode outside the walls of the Forbidden City.

"I'd like to see a eunuch," said Stone. "Doc's bin talking no end about eunuchs. Say, listen, did you know they can whatch women in their tubs 'n' everything and nobody give a whoop? When I was a kid I useter think eunuchs was a Turkish tribe. These Orientals is all queer. Say listen, Edward, d'you reckon we could tell a eunuch if we seedum?"

"I guess so," said Edward. "Let's keep our eyes open."

The Imperial City has rose-red walls and the guard-houses on the walls have golden roofs. The guard-houses are like jewels having many facets. The elaborate horizon of the roofs is like a thread on which are strung fantastic jewels—red and gold and green and turquoise blue. Dragons and strange fishes and curling waves and plumes are strung upon the fringe of the pale sky. The central gate is the great pendant on the breast of the sky; the dark door of the city is set in a square mass of red plastered wall and over the archway the lines of the gold tiles are dramatically sober. The moat at the feet of the red wall holds a clear strange dream of all these things, reflections caught in a mesh of floating lotos leaves. Above the city fly the pigeons. The owners of the pigeons apparently fit their birds with little Æolian harps. A whispered wailing of flocks of pigeons falls constantly like an intangible tuneful rain upon Peking.

"From Coal Hill you kin see right inside the city," said Stone. "Doc says the eunuchs live under the blue roof and the big bugs under the yaller roofs . . . Emerly and me and Doc had a picnic on Coal Hill. Emerly fed Cigarettes to the Chink soldiers—they was tickled to death—and she told us a crazy tale about a toob of Colgate's shaving soap that one of these Chink empress dames figured was a love dope. Say, listen, I guess Emerly ain't more'n ten years older'n me. Lots of men gets married to dames ten years older'n them. A feller at school called Jenkinson got married when he was eighteen. I guess I gotta have a speel with Dad and, if he raises hell about me being too young, I kin hand out all kinds of dope like that."

"You'd better make sure of Emily first," said Edward.

"Whaddyer mean—make sure of Emerly?" asked Stone, who was in a brave rude mood. "Emerly's crazy about me, I tell yer. She certainly was peeved when her boss moved her out of Peking."

"Crazy about you!" said Edward, who felt glad that nobody else could hear him thus debating grotesquely with a shadow. "Might as well say she's crazy about me. Don't you know who she's crazy about?"

"Aw, cut it out," said Stone uneasily.

"Didn't you see her look at Tam?"

205

"Fergit it. Tam's married. Emerly's straight, I tell yer. Emerly's not like my Mom. Any guy that says Emerly's crooked's going to hear from me. . ."

He spat angrily but neatly into the moat. Not many boys so young as he acquire so much proficiency in the characteristic arts of their native land.

Edward watched him and was afraid of him. Edward himself as a child never spat and never played roughly with the feelings of men and women. He had never dared, yet his had been a safer world.

"Emily is shameless, I tell you, Stone. . . ."

*　　*　　*　　*　　*　　*　　*

At Hankow Edward and Stone found that they had almost too much money. In order to go to Chungking—one of the few cities in the world without a Thomas Cook—they had to change their eight hundred American dollars into a much larger number of Mexican silver dollars. Their suitcases were rooted to the ground by the weight of their silver.

"Let me borrow some from you," suggested Edward, turning scarlet in a way that proved his honesty to himself. "It'll be a purely business transaction. I'll pay you two per cent per month. I want a thin suit of clothes."

"Sure, go ahead," said Stone.

Edward bought a cream-colored ready-made suit and saw in the mirror that he looked like an unsuccessful dentist. He walked hurriedly out of the store to escape this dreadful ghost.

"You look like thirty cents," said Stone, who

seemed to have inherited his mother's frank callousness.

They embarked on a wide sunny little steamer for Ichang. Edward sat on the deck day after day and saw failure gathering like a cloud about his hope of Emily. He reminded himself industriously of his hopelessness and of the fact that he looked like thirty cents. Edward never, in the whole course of his life, forgot any derogatory personal remark made about himself in his hearing. He luxuriated too much in the criticism of others to forget it.

Edward noticed the bald leathery water buffaloes at work in the flat fields; he only noticed them because he thought their faces were like his, like his own face reduced—or magnified—to the absurd. This idea made him watch for the closer buffaloes with a morbid eagerness. On the tilted swaying back of one near the tail sat a little boy in a broad hat, playing the flute and drumming his heels. The buffalo went dismally past its fellows who were lying dismally in the mud; it had not enough strength of mind to defy the little boy and give itself up to its one dismal pleasure. Black trails worn by the tears of years streaked the buffalo's face; its horns drooped awry.

The river ran so smoothly that it was like a broad road of polished golden glass. It seemed that the eyes were deceived—nothing so unruffled could pass so swiftly. It seemed to Edward that he was flashing above its still surface, the cords of the western sun had snared him and were snatching him from himself. Beneath him time and youth and the river —flowered and golden—stood still and were left behind.

A dull but hot sun laid shadeless light on the exact pyramid hills that stand about Ichang and the mouth of the Yangtze Gorges.

Edward and Stone carried their silver and Stone's ukelele and golf-clubs on to a new boat. The new boat, battling against the terrible protest of the river, thrust herself into the yellow shadows of the mountains. One could feel the muscles of the strong ship wrestling with the river. The ship swung; it advanced, it bowed sideways, it reared, it faced the fearful cliffs, it seemed to save itself narrowly from disaster every minute. The river screamed about the ship. The hot sunlight was wild with noise; the shadow of the cliffs was impregnated with terrible deep echoing. The river was a maniac prisoner between the tense leaning golden cliffs.

Curious turbulent dreams haunted the water. The surface was flowered and starred with strange boiling shapes; ominous shadows—like hands and serpents and gaping faces—were half seen beneath it; scars of foam were scored across it. The water was too wild to conform to natural laws or to find its own level. There were fifty different levels between cliff and cliff. There were table-lands and canyons in the water, and glaciers of water tilted over hidden rocks. The whirlpools were like sunken golden glass

bowls in the water. Or they were like great birds'
nests, great faery rocs' nests with eggs of cream-gold
foam spinning deep down in the nests.

Close to the cliffs, the water, in a frenzy of contradiction, flowed the wrong way. Junks could sometimes move upstream without difficulty there. All
the upstream junks clung timorously to the red cliffs;
they were towed by scores of coolies. Strings of
coolies, like beads, tawny or blue, were looped along
the bright cliffs. The ropes were tied to the masts
of the junks. Women crouched under the hooped,
humped matting that covered the junks. A down-
stream junk span down the centre of the river. A
dozen oarsmen stood on the lower deck and on the
poop stood their leader beating time frantically like
the leader of an orchestra. The chantey of the oarsmen was as thin as a hair of sound in the voluminous
voice of the river. The oarsmen swung and dipped
and bowed and fell back in time to the frenzied
baton of their leader. The junk looked dark and
nervous, dipping like a dark whale. Again it darted
heavily like a bee at the whirlpools in the water; it
made clumsy feints towards the shining sharp rocks
and the cliffs; it twisted, plunged, heeled half over,
shuddered, span round and round. Yellow waves
washed the knees of the oarsmen but still they sang.

Sometimes there were loopholes in the prison of
tumultuous noise and shadow. Sometimes the cliffs
were cloven and a tranquil and compressed perspective of sun on apparently heathery moorland and

serene red-flowering cotton trees, peered down the cleft. Sometimes the mountains fell back as though exhausted by their fighting and between broad open shores the river ran more patiently. Then there were towns and temples on the slopes. Shih-Pao-Chai, a square tower of rock, challenged the ship at a wide bend in the river. Like the shadow of the rock, like its soul or its guardian angel, a tall pagoda was built against it, with nine roofs one above the other. The nine gracious roofs were like nine branches springing from the living rock. Once there was a town in a gorge built on two shelves of a sheer ochre cliff; ladders led from one shelf to the other. Sometimes there were greater towns, their lower streets standing precariously on stilts in the river. Sometimes there were temples with curled green or yellow roofs and painted walls, looking down worn steps at the river. Once the ship tied up at sunset opposite the single line of a black slope against a fading green sky. The line blossomed into the outlines of temple roofs, bending, bristling roofs under great tiers of trees and the silhouette of a defiant griffin with plumed wings and tail.

One day the spell was broken. There were grey soldiers on the bank. There were junks full of soldiers moored to the bank. Three soldiers stood on the lowest step of a temple with their rifles aimed at Edward's eye—as it seemed. The moment seemed to call for an act of heroism. "Our hero's first thought was for the women and children," thought

Edward, calling Stone huskily as he ran behind a door.

"Crack—crack . . . crack." One report was long after the others. "A Chinese Edward R. Williams," thought Edward. When he came out of cover the brigands had not moved from their stone step. Their rifles still looked into Edward's eye across fifty yards of shimmering air. Something ought to be done about it.

"Crack—crack . . . . . crack." It was like a word in a nonsense language, a made-up word that did not convey any meaning. A secret and negligible sound.

"Crack—crack . . ." The Chinese Edward Williams failed altogether this time. Probably he had forgotten to load the thing. It would be just like him. The whine of a bullet was heard so quickly that nothing was realised except an after-taste of sound. A fountain leaped in the water.

"Now watch," said one of the ship's officers. The ship's syren cut off the end of his utterance. The syren's sound was like a warlock springing up with both bony hands straight over her head. Springing and sinking . . . springing and sinking . . . to frighten children.

Terror and astonishment wiped one of the brigands from the temple step into the river. He flashed into oblivion; his desperate hand made a little passing splash in the river. All the men on deck laughed. "That was the Edward who fell in," thought Edward, laughing a little too. "Just like him." The other two brigands ran away. The syren was such an unexpected retort. There was no declaration in the voice of the syren. Doubt made them run away.

"Gee, look at the corpses . . ." said Stone. One dead man pursued another furiously down the river. They floated on their faces, legs and arms wide-thrown. They looked like dead spiders.

"They're always fighting about one thing or another up in Szechuan," said the ship's officer in an irritated voice.

Edward thought of Emily's voice, "Oh, what a party . . ."

"She will enjoy dead men," he thought.

But there was, it seemed, peace in Chungking, at least for a few hours after the ship arrived. The junkmen were taking advantage of the peace; they were leaning out of their junks armed with poles and arresting the procession of the dead in order to take the coats and sandals that were no longer needed. The retreat of the dead was easy now and, though they had a long journey before them, they needed no supplies. The cold could not reach them now, their pitiful feet might be bare. The dead soldiers, released, fled away eagerly and joined the long humble file of their fellows.

Chungking stood in the hush that comes when one's friends have forsaken one and one's enemies have not yet come. Like panels the tall, thin, wooden houses lined the steep banks of the river. Strings of yellow fish and dried vegetables and blue garments hung across the faces of the houses. The wall framed the strangely perpendicular city. The steep steps—Chungking's only streets—were like grey gashes or scars down the town. Outside the wall stood the outcast houses on unsafe trestles; the feet of the trestles were in the water; the cleanly dressed outcast women watched the vanquished soldiers leave the city and waited for the victors to come in.

The ship was moored opposite Chungking. The town on this side was diluted with grass and trees. Green hills, grey hills, blue hills lay behind it. Groves of sharp thin trees—the cypresses that are supposed to denote the graves of poets—fitted like plumed caps upon the lower hills.

Retreating soldiers were climbing the steps on their thin active ponies. Soldiers were carrying a few of the wounded along a climbing path. The wounded were bound to poles.

"Gee, Emily'll be tickled to death," said Stone. "To see us, I mean."

On shore they asked the only white man they could see, "Do you know Emily Frere?"

"I ought to," replied the stranger. "There's only about a dozen white women up here. But I never heard of her. Sure you don't mean Miss Erica Blainey?"

Edward covered up in his mind the fact that in

a community of a dozen women Emily's name
should be unknown to any sane man. He covered
this fact up as he would have covered up the information that she wore a wig, had anyone volun-
teered it, or that she never took a bath. These were
blasphemies. Erica Blainey flickered through his
mind as an anti-Emily—thin with a pointed quiver-
ing nose and pale lips and very fair corrugated hair.

"Do you know Tam and Lucy McTab?" asked
Stone.

"Now you're talking," said the Englishman.
"He's a celebrity, isn't he? An author or what
not? He's borrowed the Worsley bungalow up in
the hills. Want to go? I'll talk to your chairmen
for you."

Four men carried each chair. They wore straw
hats like the roofs of round pavilions and blue shirts
and cotton short trousers rolled high above their
knees.

The chairmen chanted intermittently as they
walked; they kept time by means of a sort of retort-
ing chant, each man speaking rhythmically in turn.
When they wanted to change shoulders they uttered
a series of small screams or jodels. As they bent
their heads under the carrying poles during the
change of shoulders, the chair dipped and canted
alarmingly to one side. Edward each time made
the change as difficult as he could for them. He
shifted his weight; the chair leaned over; there was
a little squall of startled chatter from the balancing

chairmen. Edward resented the discomfort of the chair and, since it was bad, determined to make it worse. He tortured himself by craning out over the steep edges and watching the shining narrow rice-fields piercing the feet of the hills. The rice-fields were banked up below him ingeniously in a stairway of crescent-shaped dams.

Soldiers were everywhere. In long files they threaded the narrow mud dikes between the rice-fields. The steps on the mountain slopes, the tilted shady villages and the temples were crowded with them. They wore shabby uniforms of greenish-grey, red cap-bands, grey frayed puttees apparently wound about the fleshless bone, and bare angular ankles showing between the puttees and the straw sandals. The cobbled climbing street of one village was covered with a flat roof; every house lacked the wall on the street side; every house was like a little stage, a stage set with frightened silent groups watching the loitering and thronging soldiers. Some shopmen, with strings of perforated copper money like ornaments across their shoulders, were trying to conciliate the soldiers by selling them food. Flour sausages, coarse biscuits, dumplings, a few "Shao-ping," sold at a loss, perhaps meant a daughter saved. The soldiers were small exhausted men; their jaws hung with fatigue; their panting mouths looked square; their knees knocked together. Two of them had strength enough to beat a country boy with his own carrying-pole.

Beside the road, head downward on a flowery slope, lay a dead man. The splayed yellow soles of his feet seemed to stare at passers on the road.

Here were woods in rain, pines with soft tufted grey needles . . . here was a great view of the winding Yangtze between the wet trunks of trees. Here were safe and peaceful foreign houses.

And Lucy McTab, stiff and untidy, at the top of a steep flight of steps.

"Oh, I thought you were Tam coming. How do you do, Mr. Williams? How do you do, Stone?"

No sound of Emily running along the verandah to cry, "Edward—Edward—E-yee—E-yee—" That was her joyful noise. But there was no sound of it now. Lucy's voice without that accompaniment seemed quite meaningless to Edward.

Lucy stood awkwardly patting her hair. She was not pleased to see Edward and Stone. No plain statement could have made this more transparently clear than did her glazed politeness. Edward was seized with a panic of dumbness; he could not utter the name of Emily in this nervous, constricted atmosphere.

"Well, so you've found your way here," said Lucy. "It's a long way."

"Yes."

"I thought your father expected you to wait for him in Peking, Stone."

"Yump. I guess he did."

"This is a dreadful house to receive visitors in. Look at the furniture. Tam says it was probably all bought at the ten cent store. Still, there are advantages in living here. We can have dogs here for the first time for years. I do adore dogs. I feel . . . perfect, somehow, if there is a dog in the room. Sometimes I'm shocked to think how long I spend looking at the way a dog's hair grows on his face . . . or looking at him crossing his paws in that patient way. I just look and look."

There was a dog on the hearth, a handsome Eurasian dog. Edward crossed the room and looked blankly down on its golden forehead. One was glad when one could like anything that Lucy liked, or in any way flatter her. He noticed that she shrank as he came near her as though she thought he might kiss her or insult her.

"These Chinese," went on Lucy, "are such a weird unreasonable race. I suppose one will get used to their funny ways in time. But this fighting is dreadful."

"Yes."

"However, Tam is getting a lot of work done. He is writing a book about little wars." Her voice changed as she spoke of Tam. "It is really a treat listening to him. I often think what a pity it is that every word he says just casually to me can't be preserved. All about war and politics and . . . psychoanalysis and so on. . . . He just sits and smokes—he is an inveterinary smoker—and all these brilliant opinions pour out. People would pay to hear them, I'm sure. Perhaps I am no judge, but I really do think his book, when it is finished, will be acknowledged to be one of the most meretricious books of the century . . . you have no idea——"

She checked herself. She had forgotten to be shy and ladylike, she corrected this oversight.

"Where's Tam?" asked Stone, whose feelings seemed to be a reproduction in miniature of Edward's.

"He's gone for a walk. He adores rain."

"Where's Emerly?" asked Stone.

Lucy was silent for a moment. There was a sort of clatter in Edward's mind during her silence. "Where's - Emily - where's - Emily-where's Emily," with the hurried insistence of a telegraphic tapper. In a second it would be silenced by some tremendous fact about Emily.

"Emily's gone."

Yes, there was silence now in Edward's mind.

"Whaddyer mean—gone?" asked Stone, ceasing for a few seconds to chew his gum.

"She left—I think for Shanghai. She didn't like it much here. The climate . . . the fighting . . ."

"Did you drive her away?" asked Edward.

Lucy would not answer this. She would not say anything sincere or even hear anything sincere. She was afraid of nakedness.

"We were sorry to lose her . . . in a way," she said, fixing alarmed eyes on Edward. "But her health became so bad we could not press her to stay with us."

"Did you drive her away?"

There was a bridge of hate between her eyes and Edward's.

"Tam valued her services as secretary so much. He says he can hardly get on without her."

She would not say anything real. She was like a martyr, steeped in an ecstasy of pretence, refusing to recant.

"Well, isn't this astonishing," said the exaggerated voice of Tam. "Wonder upon wonder. First a mouse eats a hole in my bedroom slippers and then we are invaded by Californians. All in one day. I forget your name—" (this to Edward) "—but I know I love you, as it were. As for you, Stone—ever find those rainbow pants?"

This was evidently a joke, but Stone did not laugh.

Edward was surprised that he remembered Tam so well. "I must have thought a great deal about him without knowing it." Tam looked excited and unkempt. He had begun to grow a beard. The falling lock of hair across his low, nervously wrinkled forehead gave him a primitive and rather barbarous look.

"Oh, I know . . . I'm always ten minutes late in an emergency, but I know now. You're Edward, the man that Emily talked about."

"What did she say?" asked Edward huskily.

"She said you were in love with her and wished

there were more like you. Are you in love with her?"

His frankness was an affectation as was Lucy's restraint. He had a wide-mouthed, insolent way of saying these things.

"Where is she now?" asked Edward.

"Oh, I see." Tam's voice was deliberately child-like and naïve. "You're one of these people who think it's immodest to mention love. Well, well, Stone and I discuss everything we think of, from God to indigestion, don't we, old man?" He threw his arm round the impassive Stone's neck. "Emily's in Shanghai, we believe. Lucy sacked her because Emily declared her love for me."

Lucy went quickly out of the room, letting no-one see her face.

How shocking. How shocking. Emily's light defences of brave, witty dignity were torn down so easily. Emily was humiliated in the sight of the humiliated Edward.

"Well, well, there's no accounting for tastes. There's no good in refusing to admit these things. Emily's a fine, unique creature—too furiously alive for her own peace of mind. I suppose you don't want to stay here now, eh?"

"No."

"Nothing to stay for? You for Shanghai, what? Well, well, if I didn't happen to be in love with Lucy, I'd come too."

In love with Lucy when Emily loved him? "It

is because he is a cad," thought Edward. "Lucy's
thin love is the kind of love a cad values. Vain men
only live by the love of second-rate women. Emily's
love doesn't flatter Tam enough. Her love is too
insolent. She couldn't cringe. It takes an inglorious
man like me to appreciate glory. It is because I am
so wholly in the dark that I can see the light of
Emily." Edward tried to imagine Emily's eager
face, should her love and eagerness be refused. He
thought of her eyes pierced with pain, her brows
drawn together, her cheeks white, the generous expression of her mouth frozen on pale lips.

"I'll walk down to the river again with you, if
you like. I want to see some fighting. They say the
Szechaanese may march in at any minute."

"Say, what did Emerly say about me?" asked
Stone in a muffled voice. This seemed to Edward
an altogether trivial interruption.

"Said you were a bully kid, of course," said Tam.
He hugged Stone's shoulders, shook the boy
backwards and forwards and made him look
ridiculous.

"That is the manner of real men with school-
boys," thought Edward. "If I had adopted that
manner Stone would have loved me."

"D'you know what happened to me this morning?" Tam began. "Stone, listen, you'll roar over
this yarn. When I got out of my bath, I couldn't
find one of my bedroom slippers. You know the
coldness of the floors of Chinese bathrooms. My

little toe is still suffering from infantile paraly-
sis——"

"We must go," said Edward. "Stone, come."

Tam's eyes wore almost the same alarmed expression that Lucy's had worn. That expression
apparently meant that Edward was not doing what
was expected of him. He ought to have been looking eagerly at Tam, waiting with a suspended laugh
on a caught breath for the climax of the story.

"Listen to the yarn," said Tam with a touch of
asperity. "I hadn't worn the slippers since my bath
the morning before. I knew I'd left them both by
the bath tub. Their names are Abelard and
Heloïse. Abelard was there, ready for duty, but
Heloïse——"

"We must go."

"'Well, I found her at last. If you'll believe me,
she was looking into a mouse hole with her tip bit-
ten off—rape of the Sabines, what? Of course she's
disfigured for life; my big toe is frankly naked now
when I wear Heloïse, but Abelard still loves her.
You'd expect him to philander now with one of
Lucy's pumps, but——"

"Come—Stone."

"I am forced to the conclusion that Edward
doesn't love me. Most people do, really they do,
Edward. Please enroll yourself with the majority."
He came over and took both Edward's reluctant
hands in his. His voice became richer. "Old man,
old man, I know you're going through hell. Don't

think I'm unsympathetic and flippant. Listen. I want to have a long talk with you. I can tell you a lot of things about Emily that will interest you. We'll go down to Chungking together. Nobody can go on long refusing to be friends with me, can they, Stone, old man?" He released Edward and hugged Stone again.

"Aw, let's go," said Stone.

As they filed along the verandah a dreadful picture of the visit came into Edward's mind. A picture of two despicable creatures, a dirty gum-chewing schoolboy and a spotty-faced dentist's assistant arriving on a futile and ridiculous errand and being met and easily dismissed by a competent man of the world in grey flannel trousers and a tweed coat—so competent that he was not embarrassed by a five days' growth of beard.

Edward wanted to hear the "things about Emily." But he wanted still more to hurt and irritate Tam. So he would not walk down to the river. He sat sullenly in his chair. The chair-bearers ran down miles of steep steps with loud triumphant cries. The chair tilted so acutely forward that Edward had to cling to its arms. He stared down on to a strange chart of towns and river. Now and then the chair-men would put the chair down and wait for Tam and Stone who were walking. Then, in the distance, Tam's voice could be heard coming nearer, saying something like, "Well, I used to smoke Lucky Strike in California, but only as a substitute. I have a very sensitive palate . . ." or, "My finger nails grow so fast in this damp climate. I have to get Lucy to cut them. Do you know, Stone, I'd rather run a mile than cut the nails of my right hand . . ."

There was no sound from Stone. Sometimes Tam laughed very loudly—stood in the path and rocked with laughter—but the joke was apparently not Stone's.

"But this is not the way to the ship?" said Edward to the chairmen as they set him down on the edge of the river half a mile below the ship. The four men, not understanding, laughed happily.

Tam and Stone arrived. "I asked. The ship doesn't leave till tomorrow morning. You must come and seek adventures with me in Chungking. If we're killed, the English and American governments will have a glorious time registering protests. Funny, they don't seem to care a damn for us until we die. I loathe diplomats, don't you? They're always too clean for words; they wash eighteen times a day behind their ears, I believe."

CHAPTER EIGHT

I cannot bear this hour—I cannot bear it—
I cannot watch its slow and tremulous dying.
Shall I deny it—mocking my denying—?
Or shall I weave a veil of words and wear it?
Yet, having woven it, shall I not tear it
With tears? I heard a messenger come crying—
Lo, here is thy lost joy. . . . But he was lying.
The thief who stole my joy would never share it.
Then cried the messenger—*Come, cease thy grieving,*
Thy joy was terrible and exquisite,
Yet here are other joys, for God is kind. . . .
But I will pay no heed, for I am weaving
A veil of words . . . a veil of words . . . that it
May fall about my heart and make it blind.

THEY WERE in a sampan crossing obliquely towards Chungking.

"S'posing we collide with a corpse . . ." said Stone.

"You adorable kid," said Tam, and the sampan rocked as he leaned over to pull the boy's hair.

They collided with no corpses, nor with any of the sampans, loaded with retreating soldiers, coming from Chungking. The steps at the foot of which the sampan landed were moving with soldiers. A few earthenware jars stood on the lowest step, abandoned by their owners. On the beach, below the steps, a herd of beggars were raking with their fingers in a wilderness of refuse. One boy, who had committed some breach of muck-raking etiquette, was being held down by two women; his legs were being stretched by another boy and the taut muscles pounded by yet another avenger. His screams followed the travellers as they climbed the steps. There was a half open arched gate through the city wall at the top of the steps. The town within the wall was so silent that, for a long time, they could hear the screams of the beggar boy on the mud shore.

Many of the booths and the shops were shut. Shopmen with black caps and long gowns stood expectantly outside their barred doors. Tense faces looked from the leaning upper windows into the abyss of the narrow street. A closely curtained light chair was carried swiftly by, and a young Chinese woman with a frightened face pushed aside the curtains and looked out when she heard the booted tread of the three foreigners. Perhaps she hoped they were wild wicked soldiers and would see her. The houses leaned together, propped up by their own crooked shadows; a fringe of gilded shop signs swayed so low that the occasional cavalrymen had to dismount and lead their horses. Soldiers passed, all facing towards the river gate. The soldiers swaggered by the dubious, watching citizens. The soldiers looked afraid, but their mouths opened to shout confident things.

THE POOR MAN

"Buy nice ivory?" said one of the shopkeepers to Tam in a soft voice. The shopkeeper clasped his hands and bowed himself slightly towards Tam. Stone was sitting on the rough counter of a deserted booth watching the soldiers. Tam and Edward left him in the street and entered the shop when the shopman had taken down one shutter.

"This feller knows me," said Tam. "It was here I finally found the cigarette-holder that Emily wanted."

The shopman brought down various and unlikely things for their inspection, an opium pipe, a large porcelain figure, a curly animal made of dull jade the color of a shallow sea, a polished screen of blackwood. Tam fingered the porcelain figure as he talked.

"I promised you I'd tell you various things about Emily. I met her first about three years ago, soon after I had married Lucy. She and I met Emily at a theatre party. . . . I am a wholehearted man and an obstinate man; at the play I was irritated because Emily seemed so conscious of her own cleverness. I didn't want to be forced to be conscious of her. I find Lucy adorable because I am never conscious of her—she is like air to me. I am clever myself and I refuse to be distracted.ʻ Emily has once or twice very nearly succeeded in distracting me—against my will. I have been hardened against her, simply because she tried so hard. I like awfully being with her. With her I can be much wittier than without her. With her nothing ever falls flat. And Lucy was fond of her too; Lucy insisted on my bringing Emily round the world as my secretary. When that was arranged, Emily said to Lucy, 'How d'you know I won't steal Tam? What would you call that, Lucy—committing astigamy?' It shocked Lucy. Lucy's mind wears tight stays, you know. That fact makes things easier for me. She never disconcerts me. On the other hand she is often disconcerted by me. Emily never is. To me, after that sally, Emily said—'How d'you know I don't love you? What would you call that?' Somehow Emily . . . never paid back the loan of life. Emily never let me forget her. She could not believe that I could continue not to love her. If she had not been so clever I might have loved her. She put her wits between herself and me—a shining armor. She did most fatally watch me, and if there was an increased softness or success between us at any time— her eyes seemed to seize that moment and devour it, so that the moment, for me, was gone. She knows herself and everything that is happening to her too well."

His fingers seemed trying to knead the china figure in front of him. The shopman's assistant had placed two bowls of tea before them.

Something had been heard outside. Edward had not heard it. Everyone was moving. The assistant ran two stout horizontal bars across the shutters. He had not time to put up the missing shutter. He was driven indoors by the sound of running feet down the street. Even Edward could hear that sound. A strange voiceless whispering of many bare feet. Men and children ran by, all in one crowd, arms bent, mouths open, distorted, breathless faces. They made no sound except with their running whispering feet. The assistant lifted the porcelain figure as one lifts a baby and crouched behind the counter with it. The shopman stood with his eye to a crack in the shutter. Edward and Tam sat on two blackwood stools at the foot, as it were, of a ghost, a blue and green and gold mandarin coat crucified on a screen.

There was no sound anywhere.

Then there was a faint shuffling. Two soldiers came uncertainly down the street. Their uniform was new to Edward, a mustard-yellow one. They carried their rifles alertly, pointing forward. They walked with a crouching gait. Their faces looked dark and drunken.

There was another silence. Then a hum of muttering voices rose from behind closed shutters.

"Well, well, better go while the going's good," said Tam in a prosaic voice. "Where's Stone, I wonder?"

The shopman made pacifying gestures and tapped his ear. There was a very distant sound of rifle fire.

Edward and Tam leaned back against the broad coat. "Better wait here a bit. D'you want me to go on about Emily?"

"Yes."

"I don't know whether you'd want me to tell you that I have been Emily's lover. Once. Champagne makes her blessedly silly and uncaring . . . she sits smiling like a baby then . . . she is serene at last. I adore people who are tranquil, who don't compete . . . Emily, gentle, is absolutely perfect. Lucy is always gentle but she is not perfect. She is not— Emily. Well, I suppose I ought to say Emily—plus champagne. You see I tell you this to show that I am not trying to make the best of myself. It became, I suppose, harder for Emily after that. She was bad-tempered often, dull often, after that. Once she cried in public and she talked sometimes pathetically about herself to me—a thing I can't stand. I am not interested in pathos. I am not interested, I may say, in people from their own point of view, especially women. I don't see pathos in myself, why should pathos be expected to appeal to me?"

"We ought to go," said Edward. He had seen a picture of Emily crying, Emily with red staring eyes full of tears, crying, behind a wet handkerchief, to find words that might effectively array her grief before a man who was "not interested in pathos."

"Let's go," said Tam. "I wonder where Stone is. Excellent person, Stone, what? Always falls on his feet."

They walked down the deserted street. The city gate to which they first came was shut and within its

arch on the inner side was a group of soldiers of
the retreating army. Stone Ponting was leaning
against the shoulder of one of the more passive
soldiers, watching the others. Stone was spitting,
preparatory to inserting a new piece of gum. The
soldiers seemed too busy arguing to resent Stone's
close inspection.

"Bum soldiers, I'll say," said Stone when he saw
Tam. "I'd like to see our doughboys act this way.
Say listen, I saw a guy chasing off with a sack of
silver and—by golly—it split. Gee, there was iron
men all over the sidewalk and he didn't stop to pick
many ofum up. The soldiers did that forum. They
should worry. What gets me's that I came up too
late."

The argument among the soldiers ceased suddenly
as the gate was half opened. They filed through one
by one. "Look as much like Chinese infantry as
you can and we'll go with 'em," whispered Tam.
They all three passed out among the soldiers and
the man in charge of the gate did not challenge
them.

The mud beach between the city wall and the
river was crowded with soldiers; by sheer force of
numbers they were shouldering the beggars and the
outcast women out of their heritage. They had one
common desire—to get away. Every boat that
could be commandeered was over-filled with soldiers
the moment it could be brought to the beach. Each
boat pushed away bristling like a porcupine with up-

right figures and with bayonets. As the current caught the boats and swung them down the river, desultory shouts came from a distant bank upstream.

"Well, well," said Tam. "It looks as if we shall have to wait till the end of the war to get across the river. I wish I could talk Chinese and then I would ask one of these soldiers what it feels like to be so much afraid. Do you know, it may sound vain, but I don't know what fear is. I'll tell you a yarn——"

"We can get on board that boat," said Edward.

Some unexplained argument among the thronging soldiers was keeping half empty a boat which had just been brought to shore. Tam, with his arrogant Englishman's manner, pushed the soldiers apart and led his companions into the boat.

"Sailee acrossee, what?" he said in a bright charming voice to the nearest oarsman. Whenever Tam used that voice he obviously expected every face to light up with tolerance and smiles. He was accustomed to this result. His charm failed to work now. For the Chinese, boat space meant life and the lack of it death. A loud noise of protest arose from all the soldiers within earshot. Angry hands sawed the air in the direction of the three intruders. Hands pushed their shoulders. No-one was smiling.

Edward jumped quickly ashore again. He had an exaggerated terror of finding himself unwelcome.

"Hey, hey . . ." shouted Tam, for once losing his confidence. "Come back, Edward. This is an outrage. You blithering fools. Have got muchee

232

money, what? Two piecee dollar per headee . . .
three dollar . . . four dollar . . . what you likee,
blast your eyes . . ."

He and Stone were pushed on shore again. They
were ankle-deep in soft mud. The boat filled with
soldiers and was pushed off. Tam was furious. He
had been made ridiculous. They sat in a sombre
row on the steps. There was a long silence. They
watched the boat that had refused them make its
difficult way across the river. They were all half
conscious of the hope that it might be hit by a stray
bullet or two, that they might be avenged. But all
the shots went wide. White upright needles of
water showed where the shots fell, far short of the
path of the crossing boats.

"Emily did come here, though, didn't she?" said
Edward in a strained voice.

Tam's face brightened. This story ministered to
his vanity. He was enjoying the telling of it.

"Why, of course she did. She was a wonderful
secretary. If she'd wanted to go, I wouldn't have
allowed it. She didn't want to. All the way up the
river she kept up these curious fantastic moods. She
would say the most extravagantly affectionate and
admiring things about Lucy. She talked—curiously
enough—a great deal about you, Edward. You
don't mind my saying that she laughed at you a lot.
When Emily is malicious she is very amusing. That
side of her cleverness doesn't annoy me; that form
of her humor is a sort of complement to my humor

—which is essentially unmalicious. I love everyone. I really do. I love loving—so I love. So she
and I don't collide there, as it were. However, it
evidently relieved and pleased her to think and talk
a good deal of you. She had a devil's manner to
me; it was hardly bearable sometimes. She never
missed an opportunity of slighting me. She put on a
sort of disguise of sneering humility. She would
offer to go away if she were sitting with Lucy and I
came up."

Poor Emily. Edward knew so terribly well these
heartbreaking defiances of the mind. She had
sneered at him—Edward. Perhaps it had really relieved her to hide herself in sneers. Self-torturer
though he was, he could not conceive that she would
really sneer at him with her heart. He thought he
could face this possibility but actually he vaguely
imagined witty and gratifying criticism of his mod-
esty and his intensity. He only imagined mockery
from her that he could have borne to hear. He
thought, "Our selfless hero is willing to be sacri-
ficed on the altar of her pain."

Tam was saying, "Yes, of course she came here.
She was here for three days."

There was another uproar among the soldiers on
the beach.

"Gee, there's some white men in trouble," said
Stone. He jumped to his feet and hurried towards
the scene of the trouble. Two Englishmen in a
motor-boat were holding themselves several yards

from the shore. Their intention was to pick up a third Englishman who was waiting on the beach. But the intention of about fifty Chinese soldiers evidently was to board the boat as soon as it touched the shore. Everyone was angry. Tam and Edward and Stone joined the marooned Englishman on land. This re-inforcement rather disconcerted the soldiers. The motor boat drew in. Tam, Edward, Stone and the stranger flew into the air at the same second. There they were, safe in the boat. Edward had slightly sprained his ankle. A Chinese soldier was unfortunately found to be safe in the boat too.

"Push him over," said the steersman in a savage voice.

"Oh, let him stay," said Tam, laying his hand on the nervous soldier's knee. "He's equalled my long-jump record. He deserves to be preserved."

Everyone except Edward smiled and felt kindly towards Tam and the intrusive soldier. The boat made a noise like a mammoth typewriter and faced upstream.

Their laborious and slanting course brought them finally to the opposite bank near to the point at which the Ichang steamer was moored.

"I'll come on board and have a drink with you," said Tam. "No need for us to part until we must."

Whiskies and sodas stood like a bond between them. Stone wished he could really enjoy the taste of whisky. He hummed a little as though he were enjoying it, but he took his glass forward to empty it secretly into the Yangtze.

Tam and Edward stood against the railing of the steamer and watched the escaping soldiers land. The soldiers on this side seemed not very much disturbed by the fact that the advancing army was now in the city of Chungking and was firing from the walls upon the river. The fugitives on this side could not have been disturbed any more by anything. They were exhausted; they crept up the slopes limply, trailing their rifles in the mud; their mouths were open, their sunken eyes apparently shut; they made little whining sounds. Some of them lay resting, as flaccid as dead worms. A few had energy enough to impress the citizens of the town into their service. The sight of arms seemed to enchant the civilians. A long line of coolies, collected by soldiers, stood roped together in a slanting row up the steps, like cattle. Upon their sullen yet unprotesting shoulders would be placed the burdens which the soldiers themselves were too weak to carry.

Edward watched one soldier blindly seeking a human animal on which to place his pack. A child could have knocked that soldier down. He was thin and immature; he could pretend to be a man no longer; his shoulders drooped forward, his hanging head swayed between them; his eyes seemed shut; he dragged his rifle in the mud; he walked awry like a drunken man. Six big boatmen saw him coming towards them. He followed them as a senseless ghost or curse might follow, slowly and sightlessly. He followed them on to a moored junk and from that on to another. On the last junk in the line he came up to them. They would not fight; they could retreat no further. Still without seeming to see them he selected one. That one did not protest; he was driven away to be roped to the end of the growing line of cattle-prisoners on the steps.

"They'll never come back, those men," said Tam. "The soldiers shoot 'em when they're through with 'em. Poor devils."

He said "poor devils" in an intense tremulous voice, as though he were really sorry for the afflicted townsmen. Edward imagined him saying to himself, "I'm a tender-hearted chap, a man of wide sympathies. I must make that quite clear."

"People never undeceive self-deceivers," thought Edward. "We all conspire to pretend we are deceived."

Tam took Edward's arm with a roughly loving flourish and said in a brisk voice, as though brushing from his mind's eye an unmanly tear—which he was nevertheless proud of—"A heart-breaking sight, old man, let's sit on the other side of the deck."

They did so. The sharp needles that denoted rifle fire from the other side were being injected into the shining body of the river. But though even Edward could sometimes hear the mewing twang of shots in the air, it was obvious that the marksmen were giving the foreign ship a fairly wide berth.

"I'll go on about Emily," said Tam in a rather luxurious voice. "It's an unhappy yarn for me to tell, of course, but you have a right to hear it. Lucy turned her out of our house. We had been here three days. Lucy is . . . rather dumb in this story, if you know what I mean. Lucy has always escaped storms. She thinks emotions are indecent—any kind, I mean, and any degree. But especially misery or ecstasy. If you said to Lucy, 'I believe in God,' outside of a church, she would think you were irreverent. If you said, 'I love you better than my life,' outside of a decorous marriage or recognised flirtation, she would think you improper. All along you could see that she was hiding the situation from herself. But, I suppose unconsciously, she developed a habit of being obviously proud of me in Emily's presence. She had a way of looking round when I said anything clever, as if saying, 'Look what he can do—and he's mine.' Several times Emily, who never hides anything from anyone, least of all herself, commented with a sort of swagger on this trick of Lucy's. Once she said, 'Lucy, you look as if you'd helped the Lord to create him.' 'Mother Lucy's chicken,' she called me once or twice. But one night at that bungalow it was fearfully hot——"

At that bungalow! Emily's sure clear presence had really parted the pine-shadowed air of that garden. The sound of Emily's steps clicking up those steps had really travelled on this warm damp wind to an unquickened hearing.

"Lucy put her hand on my arm and said in her tolerant and reproachful way, 'My darling'—like that, 'My darling'—as a check to some flippant profanity I had just indulged in. And Emily stood up and—you know her way, even in small things—jumped with her heels on the floor. She clutched her clenched hands to her breasts and drew the corners of her mouth down and shouted, 'Not your darling—not your darling—not your darling—' many times. It seemed as if she would never stop. My God, we were all perspiring—we were so sick with heat and with disgust, somehow, even I, who am not afraid of emotions. Emily came and beat with her hands upon my chest. 'Oh, Tam'—she cried, 'Oh, Tam—save me . . .' Then you could see that Lucy had been expecting something of the sort all along—she was so quick. Lucy had her. Lucy had her fast by the shoulders. Lucy pushed her in a sort of fussy, curious, shocked way out of the room. Lucy was dark red and she was making a sort of stammering blubbering little voiceless sound between her lips like someone shooing away a hen. 'Now you can go right away at once . . .' I could hear Lucy saying in a loud trembling voice in the next room. I could hear the shuffle of Emily's things being thrown into the suitcase."

Emily's things! There was something unbearably poignant to Edward in that. That delicate fawn-colored silk dress that had held her body, the beads from her neck, the shoes from her dancing

239   Q

feet . . . all Emily's things outraged, not wanted, the things she had chosen to be part of her presence—despised.

"Lucy worked absurdly hard. She insisted on carrying the suitcases out on to the verandah; she made her insistence somehow insulting. She pulled Emily's arm as they went to the verandah, as though to make it clear that this was a forcible ejection. Well, there was nothing for it. I fetched the chair-coolies. There was nothing to be done. Emily seemed to be beyond help—she was beyond her own control; she was crying so violently, crying with a sort of grin, a downward grin, in the violent way a child cries . . ."

And now Edward was crying. He had his head upon his arms on the railing. He was crying without pretence. There was a whirlpool of helpless fury in his heart. To cry was all that he could do—because Emily had been made to cry so terribly.

"Well, well, it's a hysterical yarn altogether," said Tam. He laid his hand on the back of Edward's neck. The touch was meant to be sympathetically manly, but his fingers seemed to pinch Edward's neck almost spitefully.

"You poor thing . . . Edward . . . You're a poor thing. You poor things can never be happy. Sorrow gravitates to people like you. You—poor—thing. . . ."

CHAPTER NINE

Now I have nothing. Even the joy of loss—
Even the dreams I had I now am losing.
Only this thing I know; that you are using
My heart as a stone to bear your foot across. . . .
I am glad—I am glad—the stone is of your choosing. . . .

EDWARD thought of Emily waiting for him at
Shanghai. He had her address from Tam. He had
telegraphed to her. But surely she would know,
even without telegrams, that he was coming now.

It was a dingy hotel in Shanghai. It had brown
pillars painted to resemble marble. The resem-
blance was as faint as was that of the paper objects
on the mantelpiece to flowers.

Edward waited and waited. He had not told
Stone where he was going. Stone had gone to a
movie. Edward hoped that he would never see him
again. Edward still had most of Stone's remaining
money in his suitcase. Somehow if he never saw
Stone again Edward felt that the money would not
matter. If one were never reminded one need not
remember. A crime of which one was never accused
was no crime. Edward had no self-accuser on the
subject of money. There were limits to his humility
and to his humiliation.

241

Edward waited and waited.

Even when Emily came he found himself still waiting. For she came with a group of people.

Edward felt sick. His lips and his hands trembled. Emily did not look so incredible as he had expected. She looked quite human. He thought it was amazing that he should recognise her. How did he know she really was Emily? She was hidden in a crowd of foolish people. She was disguised by a calm rather stiff smile and faint blue shadows under her still eyes. Her body, usually nervous with life and mockery, moved staidly.

"Well, Edward . . . I got your wire. I have been dreadfully excited since I got it. You darling, funny old Edward . . . Now you must know all these nice people . . . Mrs. Thompson, Mrs. Hoskins, Mr. Thompson, Captain Ross . . . this is Edward Williams."

How little her voice was. She had probably worn it away by crying.

"Isn't it funny—I knew Mrs. Thompson when I first came out in India and she and I have been spinning round and round the world ever since without colliding—till now. They are all on their way back to India from here—much too soon for me. . . ."

That accounted for them. They lived in India. They were all accustomed to supporting British prestige.

Mrs. Thompson and Mrs. Hoskins looked bright for a moment, noticing that Edward was a man.

THE POOR MAN

Their faces fell when they saw what a poor man he was, but they did not become spiteful as they would have, had he been a woman. Mrs. Thompson cringed intensely as she shook Edward's hand; she peered with rigid sweetness into his eyes. The manner was automatic with her when a man was introduced. The hair of Mrs. Hoskins was brightly dyed and she had apparently been crushing cinders upon her eyelashes. So she did not trouble to don a laborious charm of manner; she relied upon her outside enchantments. Mr. Thompson was faded and supercilious; his withered tired face was set at an angle that directed his eyes far above anyone's head. Captain Ross' collar seemed too tight for him and his tiny moustache quivered as if he were not quite sure whether people really appreciated his importance.

Edward had been brought up as a child in India. All his mother's friends had been of this type—at least the husbands had been his mother's friends, the wives her enemies, this division being the basis of society in India.

A terrible thing was happening. Everyone was going away except Mrs. Thompson.

"Back soon, Edward," said Emily. "I must take Toby Ross to the map and make him admit that New York is further west than Valparaiso."

Two by two they went into another room, Emily and Captain Ross, Mrs. Hoskins and Mr. Thompson. Mrs. Thompson was unable to move since she

243

could not, of course, cross the room unescorted by a man. She sat down tenderly beside Edward.

"It is *so* hot . . ." she leaned forward with her face near his. The heat, he gathered, was a secret between him and her. "It is *so* hard on me to come into this heat. I suffer *so* from heat."

"Emily looks thinner too," said Edward. He felt ashamed because a face that was not Emily's was so close to his.

Mrs. Thompson looked aggrieved. "No, but it is *particularly* difficult for me. People don't seem to understand how acutely I suffer in this damp heat. I have had bronchitis *twice* in the last year. My husband is in *despair.*"

"She expects me to love her the more for her bronchitis," thought Edward. He sat and perspired. "Why live in India, then?" it occurred to him presently to say fretfully. "Why live at all?" he might have said.

"My *whole life* is bound up in India. My *dearest* friends—you don't happen to know J. L. Wilkinson of the Tea Commission, do you? Funny, I get on *so* much better with men than with women . . . In India we know how to live and enjoy life. . . . One's servants *adore* one—look how difficult the labor problem is in England—We had a house in St. Leonards when we were on leave . . . I had to open the front door myself. I often thought how *horrified* my friends in India would have been . . . a fragile person like me . . ."

Here was Emily coming, leading the procession. "I was right. Toby was wrong."

Captain Ross raised one eyebrow. The skin of his face looked so tight that one wondered how his eyebrow found leeway. Certainly he could not have moved both at once.

"Most ex-straw-dinary thing," he said in a suffocated voice.

"Sure you won't come to the Merriment for dinner, Emily?" asked Mr. Thompson. The faces of Mrs. Hoskins and Mrs. Thompson showed this plainly to be a man-like idiocy. It would have been impossible for either of them to tolerate a party at which there should be one woman too many.

"I'm dining with Edward tonight," said Emily. "Another time, please, I'd love to."

They were gone.

"Come up to my room," said Emily.

Directly the door of her room was shut behind them, Emily's face began to twitch. Her eyes looked twice as large as they had been; it was because they were full of tears.

"Oh, Edward," she cried, running to him, "you have heard. You have heard. Isn't this a terrible thing? Everything has been terrible that has happened to me. Edward . . . I can't ever stop crying. My eyes are tired of holding tears in . . ."

Edward had her at last in his arms. He sat on her bed and held her on his knee. She was rigid. She would not be comfortable. She pressed her face

245

into his shoulder but her body was stiff and uncomforted. She cried, "Edward . . . Edward . . . Edward . . . such a terrible thing . . ." Her crying sounded fantastically like laughter. She cried in a little weak downward scale, a little A-ha-ha-ha-ha . . . and Oh Edward—with each upward breath.

Edward was trembling violently. He was racked with disgust because of his own dumbness. He stroked her hair with his shaking hand. He stroked the back of her neck, her twitching shoulder. He put his lips to her hair. She was murmuring something, but her mouth was against his shoulder. What was she saying? He was cursed. His ears shut from him small epoch-making sounds.

"Emily, what are you saying? Lift up your head . . . I can't hear."

"Oh, you can't hear, you can't hear. Nobody can save me."

She slipped her shoulder from under his hand. She stood up. "There is no comfort anywhere for me," she said. She looked out of the window. She was more quiet but often her long upward breaths were sobs. "Go away, Edward. I can't dine anywhere with you. With people looking on. I can't stop crying any more."

The time for touching her was perhaps over, but he stood beside her at the window and took her indifferent hand. "I can't go away. I can't leave you alone."

"I can never be alone. That's the dreadful part. I can't get away from myself. I am horrible to myself."

"You are perfect to me."

Her hand in his trembled a little. What did she say? She spoke in such a shaking small voice.

"Yes . . . after all my lovely life . . . I am loved by you."

Could she have said that?

There was a long silence but they were standing hand in hand all the time.

"I will order dinner to be sent up here," said Edward.

"The waiter would see me crying. People would talk if I dined with a man in my bedroom."

"Listen, Emily, lie down. I will go out and buy . . . strawberries and cream . . . and asparagus . . . and cheese straws . . . and champagne . . . the most perfect things to eat and drink in the world. Couldn't you laugh again, sitting picnicking cross-legged on the floor . . . as we sat in the California forests?"

She gave a loud broken cry and threw up her hands.

"Oh, Tam . . . Tam . . . Tam . . ."

"Lie down, Emily."

"Tam . . . Tam . . . Tam . . ."

"Lie down, Emily."

She lay face downwards on her bed. He noticed that her face fitted into a depression in the pillow

247

that was already there. So she had already spent hours in that attitude.

She was still in that attitude when he came in—laden. A laden Chinese from the shop was behind him outside the door. Edward had bought thin Chinese plates patterned with green dragons; he had bought two gold-colored Venetian glasses for the champagne. He had not even forgotten a corkscrew. He spread supper on a fine Swatow tablecloth on the floor. Emily took no notice. Edward thought, "Is this silly or is it just right—to have supper on the floor? Would another man have done it differently—bought a table or something?"

He touched Emily's hair.

"Look . . . darling little Emily."

She was not crying when she lifted her face. She got up and put her arms round his neck. "Charming Edward, gentle, comforting, funny, Edward."

His name sounded exquisite like that.

When she had drunk a glass of champagne her eyes were quite dry. Neither she nor Edward spoke for a long time. Emily ate a little of everything that he had bought. But she would not keep pace with him in drinking champagne. Now he was sure he would hear everything she said; she might say some tiny perfect thing that would otherwise have escaped him. But all she said was, "Toby Ross wants me to marry him."

"Sensible feller," said Edward. He was careful to be very calm, but secretly he was rigid with anger

248

against Ross. Edward hoped that Ross was capable
of feeling the pain that he deserved.

"I suppose that would seem to you the last degra-
dation. To become a memsahib. To paint one's
face and talk malevolently about 'people not quite
of our class.' To play bridge very well and have
'absolutely *no* time to read, my dear.' To spend all
one's energies on scoring off other women. It would
certainly be a . . . flat end to all high adventurous-
ness. I met Toby in India—it seems a hundred
years ago, really six years ago. (Was I alive six
years ago? I wonder how I used my thoughts up—
six years ago.) What do you think of Toby,
Edward? Somehow I can't compare him with
other people. He hates highbrows. He is even a
little ashamed of reading Charles Lever. When he
says something that is not so stupid, I think proudly
'that's darn good for Toby.' . . . I don't know
why I feel like that. About nine out of ten things
he says prove that he has missed the whole point;
the tenth thing, well, perhaps I put the cleverness into
it myself . . . kind of defensively . . . anyway I
pretend to myself that it is a tiny bit clever. I have
been so much . . . afraid of Tam all these three
years that I thought a great deal about Toby . . .
and about you, Edward, lately. A sort of safety. I
thought, 'Well, even if he despises me, Toby and
Edward don't . . . and sometimes they are perhaps
a little bit wonderful too.' I often think of something you said about Elijah's cloak dropped by mis-

take from the flaming aeroplane and then I think, 'Why . . . why, Tam, there's a waiting list of clever men for me.' If you are despised you build walls round the last little stronghold of your vanity. Mine were weak walls. They fell down altogether at Chungking. I don't know why things have happened to me this way. I'm the sort of person, Edward, who is always said to be charming—by people who don't love me. Elderly men and kind women seem to think I'm everywhere beloved. Perhaps I swagger a bit . . . not in so many words, of course. One thing I can never swagger about, the only perfect thing in my life . . . that the most darling and wonderful man in the world . . . loved me for an hour or two . . ."

After a pause she said, "I suppose Tam is right. I am too conscious, too watchful of what is happening to me."

And then presently, "But you do love me—Edward, say quickly—you do love me, don't you?"

"I'm a very dumb person," said Edward. "It is great pain to me to be so . . . shut away from the hope of really telling you how much I love you. Emily, would you—but, please, you must—you must marry me tomorrow?"

What was she saying? Her head was on his shoulder. She spoke softly but now he could hear. He was listening and planning just as though he were a real man—not Edward. Adequate at last.

"If you leave me alone," she said, "I shall never

stop crying. Can't we go to some happier place? This minute? Edward, don't leave me alone for a minute here."

He would never leave her alone again. Everything was perfectly easy at last. He had money. Stone's money. Nothing could be more easy or fortunate.

"But she is pretending I am Tam. Never mind, I can pretend too. I have always been good at pretending. I can pretend that she wants me at last."

From minute to minute he could pretend. Not for longer. It was very dangerous. He would not face the coming minute. He could not hold the frenzied minutes. They were mad. They were frantic, thundering towards the fearful edge of the world.

Was this the happier place she had spoken of? It was the "best suite" in the happier hotel. There were Emily's two suitcases on the floor. One was leaning against Edward's suitcase. The room was panelled in pale blue. This was only the sitting-room. The bedroom opened from it.

Time was doing its best. One minute gave him Emily's—"Oh, Edward, darling . . . isn't it all lovely . . ." Another—"Let me look at you, Edward, at least you have nice heavy eyes. What would happen if you opened your eyes wide?"

Then she pushed him angrily. She put her two thin, cruel hands upon his chest. She was crying again. "Go away . . . go away. You are nothing . . . Oh, Tam . . . Tam . . ."

She had gone into the inner room and locked the door.

He was nothing. She was right. He could see himself now, sagging, disordered, his forehead against her locked door. She was speaking. What was she saying? Was she saying, "Wait, Edward, wait only a little minute . . . darling Edward, I love you . . . at last."

No, he could not hear what she was saying. He was on his knees to her locked door. "Emily . . . Emily. . . ."

She would not answer.

Yes, she answered. She opened the door. She ran past him into the middle of the outer room. She turned and faced him . . . Her cheeks were very red and her eyes excited.

"Leave me alone," she shouted harshly and hideously. "Can't you leave me alone? I can't bear you. I couldn't bear to touch you—you poor sickly thing. . . ."

That was nothing. What she had said was nothing. Silence had covered it up now. If he could put his arms about her again . . .

She hit him on the face. She hit him again and again.

She was crying again. She would not let him reach a rock of silence in this wild sea in which he was drowning. She was crying loudly. And whose voice was that, beseeching against her crying? "Emily . . . Emily . . . Emily . . ." Was it his own voice?

"You must believe it now," she sobbed. "You—poor—thing. . . ."

She was gone. The seas were still. A desert . . . a continent of silence. . . .

www.ingramcontent.com/pod-product-compliance
Lightning Source LLC
Chambersburg PA
CBHW050024180626
46810CB00002B/565